Poisonous

The 'D' #2

Charity Parkerson

Punk & Sissy Publications

Contents

Introduction

♥

CAUGHT BETWEEN TWO MEN, Abel must choose. He can unmask the man who saved him or love the one who wants him. Both choices feel equally doomed.

Six months out of rehab, Abel is relearning how to live. Mostly, life is quiet now. Some days it makes him crazy doing nothing but wandering the halls of Silas' huge house by the river. The only time Abel feels anything but apathy is when he gets clandestine visits from his secret benefactor. Then he feels very alive. Until it's over, that is, and Abel has to go back to the boredom of simply surviving.

Everything changes when Jasper bursts onto the scene.

As a successful boxer, Jasper is used to getting what he wants. From the first time he set eyes on Abel, Jasper has felt a kinship with the fire he sees in Abel's eyes. It's obvious Abel thinks there's no real hope for him. Jasper won't stop until he proves Abel wrong. The problem is Jasper is poison. He has secrets and a darkness he doesn't think Abel will understand. Eventually, the truth always wins.

Between the benefactor who saved him and the sexy boxer who won't leave his head, Abel can't find steady ground. There's something about both men he can't resist. If only they were the same man...

Chapter One

♥

THE TINY TABLE, BARELY big enough for two, kept Abel from feeling too lonely. He spaced his drink and plate far enough apart and away from him to take up as much of the table as possible, so it looked like he didn't have room for company. Over the past six months, he had gotten good at eating alone. He liked this outdoor cafe on the edge of the river in the Quarter. There were always people performing nearby to give him something to look at other than his phone. Even though Abel recognized it was completely his fault that he had no friends, it was like a whole-ass job living life by himself. Abel knew the quiet life he led now was exactly what he needed. Six months out of a three-month-long inpatient substance abuse program, and Abel felt almost human again. Unfortunately, being human meant emotions. Abel had never been good with those. He was learning, though. Mostly, that was due to Silas and Sir.

Nine months ago, Abel hit rock bottom. Addiction had owned him. He had gone to the only place he knew he could still go for help: his little brother, Griffin. While he had never been close to his brother, Griffin was a good person. Despite coming from the same abusive home as Abel, Griffin had his shit together. Abel wanted his secret to peace. Griffin sent him to Silas D. Silas was rich, eccentric, and willing to help as long as Abel gave him one thing: complete submission.

Since Abel had already failed spectacularly at living, he thought he had nothing to lose by handing the keys to his life over to Silas. Silas had immediately put those keys up for auction to the strongest dom. Sir had won him. Now nothing was the same.

Abel still lived with Silas. After all, Silas' house was like a halfway house for the weary, and Abel had nowhere else to go. He was too big of a mess to work. His anxiety spiked over the smallest things. That brought him full circle to here, eating lunch alone. Sir insisted. If Abel ate alone in public and didn't have a panic attack or give in to the temptation to use, Sir would come visit him. That was all Abel lived for any longer.

He took a bite of his salad and watched a homeless guy chase after a tourist, trying to clean his shoes. Abel couldn't stop staring as he ate. He was invested in seeing how the scam played out. With his mind busy, Abel ate without thinking too much about being alone. He had learned a long time ago that distraction helped him choke food down. His body simply didn't like doing that any longer.

"Lord, I can't take it any longer. How do you sit here without talking to anyone?"

Abel startled a bit as the chair across from him suddenly filled with a smiling male. "What?"

The guy had a glass of water in his hand. He pushed Abel's glass away and set his down—like he owned Abel's table. "You've been sitting alone for like an hour now. I can't take it any longer, so I ordered water. Now I can join you. I'm Jasper."

Jasper hadn't stopped smiling through every word. The guy screamed happiness. It was blinding. Actually, everything about him was too bright. His teeth were white. His dimples were deep. The dude had green eyes that were the color of a neighbor's grass. He was spectacular, but his presence meant Abel wasn't eating alone and Sir wouldn't visit.

"I prefer being alone."

"No one prefers being alone. What's your name?"

Since Abel didn't own the restaurant, he didn't know how to make Jasper go away. He fell back on the bitchiness that had driven away everyone years ago. "It's Abel. Go away."

Jasper snorted. "You're funny, Abel. What do you do for a living?"

Abel fought an eye roll. "Why is that always people's first question? If you plan to stay, at least be original."

Jasper shrugged and rearranged the table, making room for himself. "Fine. What's your favorite animal?"

Despite himself, Abel smiled. Jasper was too much of everything. His open happiness was clogging the air. The audacity was irresistible. "Bears."

A loud bark of laughter burst from Jasper, making heads turn their way. Normally, Abel would itch to get away from the attention, but he was oddly locked into Jasper's gaze. There was something about his eyes.

"Why bears? That seems random."

Abel shrugged. "There are so many types and they're all so different. Like, did you know there are sloth bears? They're ridiculously cute and sad-looking. Then there are black bears. Black bears don't give a fuck. They'll open your car door like a human and just jump right in." Abel had no idea why he kept talking to Jasper. It had just been so long since he wanted to speak, he couldn't resist. "What about you?"

Jasper shook his head. "No. I don't usually jump into stranger's cars."

It was Abel's turn to laugh. "So, it's just strangers' tables you hijack. Good to know. I meant animals, you weirdo. What's your favorite?"

Jasper rubbed the back of his neck. His gaze moved from side to side. The muscles in his arm flexed, fascinating Abel. Until that moment, Abel hadn't realized how cut Jasper was. "I guess I do look a bit like a weirdo right now," Jasper said, distracting Abel. "If you'd seriously like me to leave you alone, I will."

The air thickened. Abel felt a panic attack pressing on his brain. It would pounce if Jasper left. Abel forced a smile to his lips. "I want to know your favorite animal. I told you mine. It's your turn. That's the rules. I didn't make them."

Jasper's ridiculously bright smile was back. "Oh. Okay. It's turtles."

"Turtles?" Abel realized he sounded every bit as disbelieving about Jasper's turtles as Jasper had about his bears. He couldn't help it. Abel had expected something like tigers from someone as enthusiastic as Jasper.

Jasper nodded. "Turtles are cool. They're the ultimate nomads. Think about it, they're literally just backpacking it all day, every day. Their lives are one big hiking trip. That's awesome. Their homes are literally just wherever they are at that moment in life. Goals, man."

Abel's cheeks ached. It had been a long time since he had smiled for so many minutes in a row. "I get the feeling you've already achieved that level of chill. You're looking pretty at home at my table right now."

Jasper startled, as if remembering something. "Oh, yeah. You were eating. Goddamn. I should let you do that. Come see me tonight. You know, after you've eaten."

Abel was back to blinking in awe. Jasper really acted as if Abel knew a single damn thing about him beyond his name and favorite animal. "Come see you where?"

A bright smile snapped back to Jasper's lips. "You really don't know me, do you?"

"I really don't," Abel confirmed while shaking his head.

Jasper stood and dug something from his back pocket. He set it on the table. "Come see me tonight. I promise you'll be entertained." Before Abel could look at the card on the table, Jasper quickly kissed Abel's cheek and skirted away. He leapt over the short wall, separating the outdoor seating from the street. "See you tonight, Abel," Jasper called over his shoulder. He was halfway down the street before Abel recovered from his shock. No one had kissed him in any way in too long for him to recall. His body froze beneath the realization of that.

Finally, his gaze dropped to the table. The thing he had thought was a card turned out to be a ticket. Abel picked it up and read.

VIP PASS, Seat 1A, The Ironbound Arena. Cloud vs. Gordon.

Abel's brow furrowed. He picked up his phone and googled the fight. An image of Jasper, looking fierce and nothing like the smiling idiot who had commandeered Abel's table, stared back at Abel from his phone. *Jasper Cloud. 38.* Abel blinked at the words that followed: *US middleweight boxing champion 2016-present.* Holy shit. He had just been given the ultimate front row ticket to an event by the fucking US champ and Abel hadn't even known it. That was... insane.

"Do you need anything else?"

Abel's chin lifted at his server's question. He shook his head, still recovering from his shock. "No. Just the check, I think."

She smiled. "Your lunch date already paid."

"Oh." Abel didn't know what else to say. The afternoon had been weird as hell. "I guess I'm good, then." Reality set in as the server walked away and the credit card Sir had given him burned a hole in Abel's back pocket. Sir would think Abel hadn't eaten today and Abel would be punished. Either he wouldn't see Abel today because of it... or he would. Abel wasn't sure which punishment would be worse.

He kept little cash on him since he didn't have a job, but Abel left what he had on the table as a tip. Abel didn't know if Jasper had tipped, and he couldn't leave the server nothing. It hurt his chest a bit to leave the last of his money, though. His anxiety spiked as he walked away. Without that last few dollars, he completely depended on the kindness of Sir. That was beyond terrifying.

"Excuse me."

Someone touched his arm, drawing him up short and sending his inner panic through the roof. He turned to find the blond server at his side.

She held his money out to him. "Your date left me a huge tip and asked that I not let you leave one too."

Abel drew a breath. As air filled his lungs, he realized how close he was to a full-blown panic attack. He had been holding his breath without even realizing it. "Thank you."

His hand shook as he reached for the money. He didn't meet the woman's gaze to see if she thought he was as fucked up as he was. Instead, he took his last few dollars and practically ran. To most, eight dollars was nothing. For Abel, it was all the money in the world that truly belonged to him.

With his head down, Abel barreled his way down the sidewalk, navigating the city purely on memory. His thoughts raged now that he was alone again. Thoughts jumped from topic to topic, always coming back to Sir. Maybe he should pick up something to go from a different restaurant so Sir wouldn't find out about lunch. That was dumb. Sir always knew. He knew everything. It was like he was everywhere. Abel stopped outside a closed shop. It was as nondescript as the rest, but special to Abel. His brother was inside.

Abel tapped on the glass door. Griffin turned. He was all smiles when he caught sight of Abel. Abel didn't deserve it. Griffin was simply a cinnamon roll who couldn't have the happiness beaten from him. The way Abel had.

Griffin practically bounced to the door. His eyes danced with kindness as he let Abel inside the future home of Andrew's art studio. "Hey, sweetie. I wasn't sure if you still planned to come by today."

Abel stepped inside and pasted a fake smile on his face. "Of course. It just took me a little longer than I expected to get lunch." He looked around. It was just a large room and obviously still in the works. He could tell there was some method to the madness. A few of Andrew's paintings were already on the wall. Otherwise, if Abel hadn't known it was the future home of an art studio, he wouldn't have known. Still, he humored Griffin.

Abel spun in a circle. "Things are coming together."

Abel couldn't see it, really, but he believed in Griffin.

Andrew appeared from a back room and swept Griffin against his chest. "Hey, Abel. What do you think of the place? It's not much yet and I definitely won't be quitting Assets anytime soon. But maybe one day I'll get there."

At one time, Andrew and Abel were supposed to marry. Abel saw now how lucky they had both been when they escaped that fate. Andrew looked so much happier with Abel's baby brother. Abel didn't have the patience it took to wait for someone else's dream to come true. That probably made him a bad person. Hell, he *was* a bad person. Nonetheless, they had escaped a dark future.

Abel tried to fake like he wasn't dead inside. "It'll happen. With my brother at your side, there's nothing you can't do." That was one thing Abel believed from the bottom of his dead heart.

Griffin was the strong one. He wouldn't stop until Andrew's dream came true.

Abel turned away from their open happiness and eyed the room. "This is a great spot for a gallery. You got super lucky with the location."

"Not really," Andrew said behind him. "Silas has had his ear to the ground for a few months, looking for the best spot. You know how it is. He has all the best connections."

Abel nodded while keeping his face turned away. "Do y'all need help with anything?"

Griffin tackle-hugged him, catching him off guard. "Nope. We just wanted you to see the place. You're family."

Griffin was being loving, as always. He was including Abel, as always. Griffin was reaching out to him, as always. All Griffin asked of him in return was the bare fucking minimum. Abel felt like he was failing anyhow, as always.

He tried harder to smile. It physically hurt. "Well, everything looks fantastic, and I couldn't be prouder. You two are doing great. When are you getting married?"

Silence met his question. Abel finally looked at them head on. They stared back. Realization struck. "You've already gotten married." Without him. He actually deserved that one, he supposed.

"We'd planned to tell you," Griffin said, sounding torn between happy and concerned.

Abel tried desperately to bring back the unnatural smile. They should leave him out. That was fair. "No. It's okay. It's not about me. I'm happy for you." In a lot of ways, it was true. Abel was just sad for himself. Even though Andrew wasn't meant for him, the old Abel was still inside of him somewhere, crying out for all that he had lost while he had been too strung out to care. There was a tiny part of him that wasn't dead yet and it wanted the apple pie future he had thought he would have with Andrew. Abel wasn't meant for that life. His gaze dropped to his watch as it reminded him to breathe. Another gift from Sir, tracking him throughout the day. He had to get out of there.

"I should go. I'm running late for everything today."

"Of course." Griffin still sounded bright, but it wasn't as real now.

Abel tried fixing things. "Seriously, guys. I'm thrilled for you. You are perfect for each other and all that. I'm only disappointed I wasn't there to see it."

Griffin hugged him again. "If it makes you feel better, no one was. It was a spur-of-the-moment thing. We haven't really told anyone. It's still new and has been kind of like our little secret. Something just for us."

"As it should be," Abel said, feeling the words from the bottom of his heart. He tucked a piece of hair behind

Griffin's ear. Abel knew Griffin didn't believe it, but he was the only person in the world Abel felt anything for any longer. Everything inside Abel was almost completely dead. There was a tiny hint of love for his baby brother, though. He kept trying to kindle it and bring his heart back to life. Abel didn't spare a glance for Andrew. It didn't matter who brought Griffin happiness, as long as his little brother was happy. "I'll see you back at the house. The place looks great."

Griffin's smile turned genuine again. "Okay. Be careful going home."

"I will." Abel rushed out without trying to look as if he ran away. He had spent too much time in public today. His skin itched. Abel picked up his step as he got closer to home. Sometimes, the walls of Silas' house felt like they would close in on him. Other times, they felt like the only safe space he had left. Their sanctuary kept him sober. Today, he needed the protection.

As he came to the gate of the stone wall surrounding a hidden paradise, Abel took a steadying breath. He was almost there. After punching in the code on the security panel, he pulled the gate open and slipped inside before pulling it closed again. The four-story mansion that waited for him always took his breath. It had been built in a time when things were built completely by hand and made to last. Despite its age, the house looked brand new. The beautiful landscaping made Abel feel like he had stepped back in time to when grand house parties were the only entertainment for the rich. Abel could breathe here. As he opened the front door, the scent of old wood and lemons overcame him. The huge foyer opened to a large spiral staircase—like something from a gothic fantasy.

Silas had one foot on the bottom step as if Abel had caught him heading up. Today, Silas looked as normal as a man with endless funds could look. He wore a t-shirt and jeans, but they did nothing to hide a three-hundred-dollar haircut and fifty-thousand-dollar watch. His hair was grayer than any other color it had once been. Silas' blue eyes were kind as they landed on Abel.

"Abel. You're late. There's a guest waiting upstairs for you. You should prepare yourself."

Abel flashed Silas a grateful smile, even though he couldn't tell if Silas' words were a warning or if he was just passing the information along. "Thank you."

Silas stepped aside and let Abel head up first. With his head down, Abel climbed the stairs. A small part of him fought the urge to jog. There was only one person who visited him. Not only was Abel late for their appointment, but there was also that business about lunch. For once, Abel didn't know what would happen when he faced Sir.

As he reached his bedroom door, Abel took a steadying breath. An eye mask hung on the doorknob, the way it did every time Sir visited. His benefactor wished to remain anonymous. If Abel wanted to keep his backing, he had to honor those wishes. Every time he set eyes on the satin blindfold, he considered disobeying. Then he remembered he had nowhere else to go, and he slipped the black piece over his eyes, ensuring he couldn't see a thing before blindly fumbling his way into the room. Abel took a few careful steps inside before closing the door behind him. He knew from trying to peek in the past that his room was plunged into darkness. His senses were heightened. The scent of expensive and manly cologne washed over Abel. He drew the scent into his lungs. Damn. Delicious.

"You're late."

Abel crossed his arms to keep his hands from shaking at the husky-sounding admonishment. Then he realized the move made him look defensive, and he uncrossed them. "I stopped by to see my brother-in-law's new art studio." Fuck. It felt weird calling Andrew his brother-in-law.

"There was no charge on your card for lunch today."

"Someone else paid for my lunch today."

"Who?" A low growl tinted the question.

Abel refused to lie to save himself. "Some guy who sat down with me while I was eating. I didn't invite his company."

Silence met his confession.

He fought the urge to squirm and rip off his mask.

Finally, Sir sighed. "So, you finally made a friend. That's fine. Come here."

Abel shuffled closer. He moved slowly toward the chair where Sir always sat. The last thing Abel wanted was to fall, but he knew from experience he would have to find his way blindfolded, with no help.

When he got close, Sir snagged his waist and lured him closer. "Tell me about your new friend," Sir demanded while going to work on unbuttoning Abel's jeans.

Abel's heart rate kicked up. He hadn't dared hope Sir would touch him today. Abel had honestly thought he would be punished instead. His body was already hard in anticipation.

Abel tried to think. He didn't want Sir to stop because he wasn't obeying. "Um. His name is Jasper. He's a boxer."

Sir kissed his stomach. He slowly set Abel's erection free. Abel reeled. Sir led Abel's hands to rest on his shoulders. It was the only place he was allowed to touch Sir. He could be old or young. Short or tall. Skinny or not. Abel didn't know or care. Sir had what Abel needed to stay sane and sober.

"What else?" Sir punctuated the question by licking Abel's crown.

Abel sucked in a breath. "He left me a ticket to his fight tonight."

"Will you go?" Sir swallowed his cock.

The thread of their conversation disappeared. He had never met anyone with a more talented mouth. It was strange. Looking back on the last nine months, and the time he spent with Sir, before and after rehab, Abel couldn't say how or when they had fallen into this unique relationship. They hadn't discussed these encounters. One day, they had gone from Abel telling Sir all his problems while blindfolded to Abel being rewarded for good behavior with a blow job. It had been an oddly normal transition. The mystery and anonymity of their relationship gave Abel this sense of nothing being real. He could take his reward without guilt or consequences. No one got hurt or had expectations. It was like their encounters never happened. Except

Abel couldn't survive without them and with every single one, Abel got more attached.

"You're not answering me."

Damn. Sir's voice sounded so husky and turned on. Abel didn't want him to stop. He scrambled to recall what they were talking about. "I don't know if I should."

Sir deep-throated him, and a moan vibrated from Abel's chest. An overwhelming desire slammed into Abel. He wanted to be kissed. Abel missed being held and petted. He missed intimacy. Sometimes, Sir scared Abel. It was like he knew how to reward Abel in just the right way to keep him clean. But he also knew how to withhold the right amount of affection to make Abel long for a normal life. It was frightening to think he could heal. Once he was whole, he would have to face the destruction he wreaked during his years of addiction. He would have to make amends. Abel would have to live again. The thought alone terrified him.

Sir's fingers dug into Abel's skin as Abel's muscles tensed. The world slipped away. His problems disappeared. Nothing mattered but the hot, perfect suction on his cock. He fought the urge to massage Sir's skin and pull his hair. Abel didn't want him to stop.

Pleasure coiled inside, winding tighter. Abel held his breath. A cry tore from his throat as his orgasm ripped through him, nearly buckling his knees. Sir kept sucking, stealing every spasm and drop of cum. Abel shook in Sir's hold. The world spun, making Abel realize he had stopped breathing. He sucked in a deep breath. It sounded painful, even to his ears.

Sir stood and eased Abel into the chair. The transfer always happened too fast and while Abel's mind was a mess, so Abel couldn't judge Sir's size. Sir leaned close to Abel's ear. His breath brushed Abel's skin. "Go play with your new friend tonight. You're ready."

Abel tried to respond, but the door clicked closed and he knew he was too late. Even though Sir's heavy presence was gone from the room, Abel kept to their deal. He slowly counted to sixty in his head before removing the mask. Even once he could see again, Abel didn't move. As always, his encounter with Sir left him shook. He was left empty.

Chapter Two

♥

HIS MUSCLES AND HIS face stung where Gordon landed a lucky blow. Jasper held on to his belt. He had known he would. Maybe it was cockiness, but Jasper didn't think so. He was too mean to lose. Gordon had heart, but crazy won every time, and Jasper was one hundred percent insane. Rage owned him despite his win. Abel's seat had remained empty throughout his bout. Jasper had told him to come. Disobedience wasn't an option. Now Jasper had to find another way to get to him.

By the time Jasper made it through his after-fight interviews and meeting-the-fans bullshit, he had to sneak out the back to avoid more autographs. There was always a seventy-five percent chance he would still run into a crazed fan, but he was extra careful tonight. His mood was shit. Jasper's mind wouldn't let go of Abel. He was an obsessive bastard and Abel had misbehaved. Now he was backed into a corner. That was always when Jasper came out swinging the hardest.

"So, Jasper Cloud, thirty-eight, native of New Orleans, Louisiana, do you always use your championship status to buy strange men lunch?"

A smile snapped to Jasper's lips. His dark mood vanished in an instant at the sound of Abel's voice. He turned. Abel leaned against the wall next to the back door. "There's no way you knew I would leave this way."

"Not true," Abel said, straightening away from the back door. "I may be a complete mess and too nervous to attend a huge event alone, but I'm observant. While watching the place and trying to decide where to go in or if I even should, I saw the other official-looking people come out this door. I hedged my bets."

Jasper took a steadying breath, hoping to keep the darkness at bay. Abel was too sexy. Jasper wanted to touch him. His dark hair begged for Jasper's touch. His green eyes bordered on brown, but when he stepped into the sun… perfection. Jasper had never been so immediately stunned by anyone the way he had been with Abel. Some might say it was because he felt like he looked in a mirror when he looked at Abel, and Jasper was a full-on narcissist. No matter the reason, Abel belonged with him.

"I'm glad you waited. It would've been better if you'd come inside. How am I supposed to wow you with my manliness now? Fighting is all I have."

Abel shook his head and stuffed his hands in his pockets. "You don't want to impress me."

Since he didn't want to hear Abel make excuses, he jumped topics. "How did you get here?"

Abel looked more uncomfortable by the second. "The same way I get everywhere. I walked."

That was good. He motioned toward his nearby BMW i8. "Get in."

Abel didn't budge. "As much as I'd like to say I haven't lived this long by being stupid, that isn't the least bit true. Still, I don't think I should get into a car with a stranger."

Jasper held his arms out, trying to look as innocent as possible—split lip and all. "I'm not a stranger. I'm Jasper Cloud, baby."

With an eye roll, Abel moved to the passenger side. "For the record, I'm not leaving with you because you're Jasper Cloud."

As Jasper moved to the driver's side, the doors automatically unlocked. He smiled at Abel over the roof of the car.

"I know. You're leaving with me because I'm fun and you desperately need that in your life."

Abel's mouth lifted in one corner like he didn't want to smile but couldn't completely fight it. "Maybe."

Jasper winked. "Get in, darling. You won't regret it."

The way Abel shook his head as he opened the door screamed he wasn't as sure, but he got in. Jasper had him now. While Abel climbed into the car, Jasper stepped to the back and dropped his gym bag in the tiny trunk before returning to the driver's side. As he ducked into the car, Jasper didn't bother hiding his smile. Abel was already seat-belted in and holding the bear that had been strapped into his seat. With the bear between his hands, Abel turned the stuffed animal from side to side, eyeing the realistic-looking toy.

"Is this a Sri Lankan sloth bear?"

A sharp laugh burst from Jasper. "Damn. You're good. I bought him for you."

Abel looked his way. Shock etched his features. "You bought him for me. Why?" Even as Abel asked the question, his hold tightened on the stuffed animal. Abel didn't realize how much his actions gave away his every thought.

"You said bears are your favorite. I thought, if you actually showed up tonight, then you deserved a gift."

Abel's gaze moved back to the bear. "Thank you. He's adorable."

Jasper started the car to stop himself from saying anything dumb. Abel sounded ridiculously moved by such a small gift. That said way too much about his life. Jasper scared himself sometimes. It was best to stay quiet. He drove four blocks through the darkened streets. The quiet inside the car felt comfortable.

Abel broke it. "What sort of famous boxer has a match and then drives home in complete silence? Shouldn't you be out, spraying people with champagne and riding an adrenaline high?"

Jasper nodded. He supposed that was as good of an opening as he would ever get. "Most likely, but I'm a recovering alcoholic. I have to avoid triggers—like big celebratory parties." He flashed Abel a tight smile. "Otherwise, I might wake up four states away with my bank account drained and half dead."

The silence that met his words was very telling. Abel understood that wasn't a hypothetical situation. Jasper had done that once.

Still, Jasper couldn't take the quiet any longer. It didn't feel comfortable anymore. "You're being awful quiet. Did I scare you?"

"No." Abel's answer was soft and spoke to something deep inside Jasper. That singular word screamed understanding and acceptance. From the corner of his eye, Jasper could see Abel fidgeting with the bear. "I guess I should probably admit I'm a recovering addict. Very newly recovering. I've only been out of rehab six months."

Jasper was proud as hell of Abel for how he said the words. His voice didn't shake. He owned his past. Jasper nodded. "Six months is awesome. It sounds like you're doing great. I'm about eight years sober now. It's always there in the back of my mind, but I'm all about winning these days. I was as low and as bad as a person could get. Trust me when I say you've absolutely got this. I can see the strength in you." Jasper pulled into his driveway and a black gate swung open, allowing him to navigate the remainder of the drive. His garage door opened as the gate closed behind him.

"Is this your house?"

The garage door closed behind them. "Yeah."

"I live just down the street."

Jasper pasted on a bright smile as he looked Abel's way. "I know. I've seen you out walking. You live in the house that has all the huge sex parties."

Abel blushed and looked away. "If that's why you approached me, you're about to be disappointed. I just live there. Those aren't my parties."

Jasper fought the urge to touch Abel's chin and bring the man's gaze back to his. He was a little scared of what might happen once he set his hands on Abel. "I'm not disappointed. I just told you I have to avoid triggers like huge parties. It's a relief to know you're not holding them."

Abel looked his way before quickly dropping his gaze back to his lap. Jasper didn't miss his shy smile. "That's good. Not the triggers thing." Abel winced. "Sorry. I'm out of practice talking to people. I hope you know what I mean."

Damn. He was perfect. "Yeah. I know what you mean." And one day soon, Abel wouldn't wince and blush anymore when he spoke. Jasper would make sure of that.

·♥·♥·♥·♥·♥·

Abel had no idea what to make of Jasper. He wanted to squeeze the bear to his chest. Abel didn't know how the guy had found a stuffed replica of the exact bear they had discussed at lunch. There was something strange about the entire situation, but he couldn't put his finger on it. Sir had told him to go to the fight tonight. Abel still hadn't figured out why. Whatever the reason, he hadn't been brave enough to go inside. He would have to admit that to Sir and take his punishment. Now that he was alone with Jasper, he wished he had made it inside the building. Abel wanted to know Jasper better. Jasper seemed genuinely nice.

Together, they stepped from the car. Jasper led him inside. The place was newer than the home where Abel lived. The neighborhood was a hodgepodge of old homes that survived Katrina with repairs and new homes built on the bones of the destruction. When they stepped through the door, the place smelled like cinnamon. Side by side inside the mudroom, they took off their shoes. As they headed into the kitchen, Abel looked around. The appliances were huge and stainless steel. They skirted a giant island with a sink in the middle and headed into what looked to be the living room. The entire place felt empty. Their footsteps echoed on wooden floors, as if there wasn't a stick of furniture in the house. In fact, the only thing in the room was a small uncomfortable-looking futon.

Jasper plopped down on it. He patted the empty spot beside him. "I know it doesn't look like much, but it's pretty comfortable. Have a seat. Oh." He brightened as he flipped down part of the futon and it became a cup holder. "It even has cup holders."

In spite of himself, Abel smiled. Jasper was just so damn positive. He was like a hyperactive and lovable dog. Abel crossed the room and sat gingerly on the futon. It was so small, and Jasper seemed so much bigger than life, Abel half expected the furniture to collapse with their combined weight.

Abel glanced around at the bare walls. "Um. Don't take this the wrong way, but why is your house empty?"

A sexy laugh rumbled from Jasper's chest. "I'm not insulted. All my stuff is back in Vegas, where I've been living the past few years. I decided to move back home and bought this house a couple of weeks ago. I'd hoped to be completely moved in by tonight's fight, but the moving company is behind schedule." He made a helpless gesture. "So I just bought a cheap, throwaway futon and I'm making the best of things."

"That's what you do, isn't it? Make the best of things. I've never met anyone so upbeat."

"Would you like me to be someone else?" Jasper's features hardened. His sharp angles made themselves known. The air in the room changed. Abel squeezed his bear. His gaze moved over Jasper's features. He focused on the bruises that were slowly making themselves known and Jasper's split lip. Abel needed to see Jasper's weaknesses. Jasper felt too powerful.

"Your face looks like it hurts."

A smile exploded across Jasper's features, bringing back the playful puppy. "You could kiss it and make it better."

Abel's stomach cramped with want. He held the bear even tighter. "You don't want that. I'm poisonous."

Jasper's forehead furrowed. "So you're saying, if I lick you right now, I'll die?"

Abel smiled. Jasper was just such a smartass. "No, but if you let me in your life, I'll eventually bite you and ruin it."

"So you're venomous?"

Abel rolled his eyes. "You're an idiot."

Jasper's bright mood didn't falter. "Probably, but I'm poisonous too. Personally, I think our negatives will cancel each other out. If not, what a ride!"

Abel stood. He wasn't ready for this. Jasper was too nice. Abel had already wrecked one nice guy and driven him into the arms of his brother. "I should go. It's just a short walk from here. Thank you for the bear."

Jasper jumped to his feet. "I'll walk with you."

Abel backed away. Panic pressed on his brain for no reason whatsoever. "That's not necessary. I'm used to walking alone all the time."

Jasper linked his arm through Abel's and steered him toward where they had left their shoes. "You're not by yourself tonight, so there's no reason to walk alone. No arguing."

Abel couldn't explain why he couldn't argue with Jasper after his simple command. Jasper hadn't put any heat behind his order. He wanted to say there was just something about Jasper. But Abel feared there was just something about himself. He needed someone to control him. Otherwise, he would spiral. He just wasn't strong. That was how he found himself holding Jasper's hand while he walked home. Abel simply handed power over to the first person willing to take it.

Warmth seeped into his chest. With their fingers intertwined, Jasper kept playfully bumping against him, as if trying to run him off the sidewalk. Abel kept his head down to hide the way he couldn't stop smiling. Jasper was a ball of sunshine. He made Abel happy. It didn't take them long to reach Silas's house. They stood outside the gate for longer than necessary. Abel wasn't sure if he wanted to be kissed or not. Sir had given him permission to make a friend. This didn't feel like friendship. Abel couldn't afford to lose the power relationship he had with Sir, and it wasn't all about the financial support.

Sir kept him sober. Abel didn't think he would stay that way without him.

Jasper bent and met Abel's stare, making a show of forcing Abel to look at something other than the ground.

With a laugh, Abel lifted his chin.

Jasper brightened. "Ah. There you are. You have a great laugh. Very musical. Now tell me goodbye so I can go ice my face."

"Goodbye so I can ice my face," Abel dutifully repeated.

Jasper clutched his chest. "Ohhh. Stabbed by the mocking sword."

Another chuckle escaped Abel. He wasn't ready to leave Jasper's company, but he knew it was time to go. "Seriously, go ice your face."

Jasper nodded. "Tomorrow, right here at noon. I'm taking you to lunch."

Abel nodded without thought even as a hint of guilt wormed its way in. He wished he could ask Sir's permission first. Abel doubted he could ask Jasper to wait while he texted his benefactor. "Noon," Abel agreed as he backed toward the gate.

Jasper moved so fast, Abel didn't see him coming. He shot forward and pressed a quick kiss to Abel's lips. Jasper backed away just as fast. "That's all I can offer with this split lip.

Thanks for showing up, even if you didn't make it inside."

Abel tried not to blush or want too much. No one understood as well as he did he wasn't relationship material. He had nothing to offer anyone, much less someone like Jasper. That didn't stop his stupid heart from doing somersaults. A breeze kicked up and ruffled his hair. For a moment, he swore he caught a whiff of Sir's cologne. It was enough to bring Abel back to reality. He wasn't free.

"Goodnight, Jasper." With those words barely gone from his lips, Abel practically ran away. He didn't look back.

Abel was more thankful than words could express when he didn't run into anyone on the way to his room. His steps slowed as his feet hit the third floor. He half expected to find a mask hanging on the doorknob, even though he had already seen Sir once today. The doorknob was empty. With a shake of his head, Abel dug his room key from his pocket. For a moment, he stared down at the expensive-looking leather key chain with a number two stitched in the center. It was the same key chain Sir had given him the night he had taken control of Abel's life. Sir had handed him the key and assured him that even though he would stay with Silas, no one else had a key but Sir. He was Sir's property. Silas was only holding on to him because Sir didn't live in New Orleans and couldn't watch him full-time.

Abel stuck the key in the door and turned the knob. It was just a key. He could give it to Silas and walk away from this place anytime he wanted, forgetting Sir. Then again, he couldn't. Abel had been given thirty-two years on this earth alone to prove he could handle life. Only his thirty-third year had been worth living, and that was when he handed control to Sir. Some people shouldn't be in charge of anything. Not even their own breathing. Abel was one of those people.

With that depressing thought at the front of his mind, Abel carried the bear to the same chair Sir had left Abel in earlier. Abel left the bear behind and moved to the dresser. He avoided his reflection in the mirror above it while he emptied his pockets. He froze as he dropped what little he possessed on top. His gaze skirted the items on the dresser. There was nothing but a gorgeous wooden clock and an empty jewelry box. Neither item belonged to Abel. They were owned by Silas. Abel didn't need to look around the room to know Silas owned everything in it except Abel, the things had just taken from his pockets, the bear, and the things Sir had given Abel. Those things belonged to Sir, as far as Abel was concerned. Sometimes, from nowhere, Abel lost his breath at the reality of his life—like being punched in the chest. Before Silas had agreed to help him, Abel had literally been sleeping in the street with nothing left to his name but the clothes on his back. He didn't know how he had gotten so bad. It had been nine months since Silas had taken him in and still most days nothing felt real. Abel always felt very detached from reality. Until tonight.

Abel took a breath. For a moment tonight, Abel had felt normal again. He had just been a guy on a date. Damn. Abel's shoulders fell. He wished he hadn't been too weak to watch Jasper's match. An idea struck. Abel quickly kicked off his shoes, grabbed his phone, and climbed into bed. He opened the web browser on his phone and searched for highlights of tonight's fights. There were a few news highlights and a YouTube video already. Abel clicked on the video. The person recording everything was obviously too far away from the ring to get anything good, but they caught amazing footage of Jasper making his way toward the ring. He wore a black and red satin robe. His face was set. Abel paused the video and stared at Jasper's expression. He looked like a different person. Despite his usual upbeat personality, Jasper possessed some of the harshest and sharpest lines Abel had ever seen. He looked like he had been carved from marble. Jasper looked deadly. Abel imagined Jasper scared people who might land on the other side of his punch. He fascinated Abel. Abel curled onto his side with his gaze still locked on Jasper's face. Damn. He hoped Jasper really showed tomorrow for lunch. Abel hadn't felt this way in a long time and Abel was an addict all the way to his core. He always wanted more.

Chapter Three

♥

JASPER WAITED ON THE sidewalk for Abel. He had shown up ten minutes early because that's just who he was, and it had been a long night on that hard futon. It had only been two minutes since Jasper arrived and Jasper was already losing patience. His mood was shitty today. He hated when his life was in upheaval. As much as he despised himself for his inability to take it any longer, Jasper might have to make a trip back to Vegas and light a fire under his moving company personally. He needed his bed. His gaze slid toward the house where Abel currently stayed. Maybe he could borrow Abel's bed for a while. Jasper closed his eyes and shook his head. He needed to ditch his dark thoughts.

"Why are you shaking your head?"

Jasper's eyes shot open, and a smile snapped to his lips at only the sight of Abel. He chuckled. "Sometimes, I forget people can see me. I was trying to shake off this slight headache that won't go away."

Abel closed the distance between them. "Here." He clasped Jasper's face between his hands and kissed Jasper's forehead. "Now you should be all better."

Jasper's breath caught in the back of his throat. It was the first time Abel had touched him without prompt. He also looked happy today. Jasper fought the urge to pull Abel against him and claim his mouth. Abel looked gorgeous. He was also all smiles, which was like a breath of fresh air.

"You're all the medicine I need. Where would you like to eat?"

Abel made an uncomfortable looking shrugging motion. "What types of food do you like?"

"All foods," Jasper said honestly. "Seriously. All of them. I'm like an empty cavern."

After glancing around, as if trying to think of which direction to go, Abel motioned toward the river. "There's that place next to the mall that has the huge burgers."

Jasper blinked. "That's one hell of a walk."

A sexy chuckle rumbled from Abel. "I thought you were a boxer. Aren't you supposed to be in shape?"

"Yeah," Jasper said, still horrified. "But I'm not trying to walk an hour to get lunch. Do you really walk that far just to eat?"

Abel shrugged, looking uncomfortable. "I don't really have much of a choice. It's not like I do it every day, but yeah. If I need to go to the mall or something, I have to walk."

Jasper's anger spiked. He tried to keep a hold on it. "Do you go alone? There are a lot of empty buildings and homeless in that area. You shouldn't be doing things like that by yourself."

Abel glanced behind him toward the house, as if he thought about abandoning their lunch plans. He rubbed his arm and shifted from foot to foot. "I don't have anyone to go with me. We don't have to eat there. It was just a suggestion. You should pick. I don't know what you want."

Abel looked on the verge of tears. His open agitation punched Jasper in the chest. Jasper had to take control. "Stop."

At his barked order, Abel's gaze slid his way.

Jasper took Abel's hand and steered him away from the river and toward

Jasper's house. "We'll take my car so we can go wherever we like."

Abel didn't say a word. He simply followed Jasper's lead. Jasper bumped shoulders with Abel, trying to lighten the mood, but Abel only flashed him a pained smile. He had to turn things around.

Jasper snapped his fingers and skipped. "I know exactly what we should do. Come on." While still holding tightly to Abel's hand, Jasper took off running. Abel laughed as he fought to keep up. As they reached Jasper's house, he headed straight for the garage. Now that he knew what to do to make Abel smile, he couldn't get moving fast enough. He rushed Abel into the car and ignored Abel's questions about where they were going as he drove across town. Jasper looked Abel's way as he pulled into the parking lot of the huge arcade. A smile snapped to Abel's lips as he eyed the building. Jasper knew he had made the right choice.

"We can eat while we play," Jasper said as he killed the engine.

Abel made a helpless gesture. "Sounds great."

Childlike excitement had Jasper jumping from the car. Hand in hand, they made their way inside. Jasper spent a small fortune filling game cards for them. They moved from machine to machine, racing each other, fighting each other, and playing Skee-ball side by side. Jasper ordered them food. It was junk like fried cheese sticks and wings. After they ate, they were right back to winning as many prize tickets as possible. They spent nearly an hour trying to win a gift card from a claw machine. In the end, they gave up and cashed in their tickets. Jasper waited patiently while Abel picked his prize. It gave Jasper time to stare at Abel unfettered. He was beautiful. Abel was a bit too skinny, but Jasper would work on that. He knew a lot about making someone well. After all, Jasper had fixed himself. He could build Abel into someone strong. Abel already had the foundation. Jasper wanted to put Abel in his pocket and keep him. He wanted to take him out and play with him whenever the mood struck. Jasper was very aware that he was controlling, manipulative, and twisted. He was also selfish. Jasper never denied himself anything. He wanted Abel, so he needed Abel well. There was no low too low for Jasper. One day, Abel would see that.

Abel glanced his way and smiled as the guy behind the counter handed Abel a bag full of candy and cheap prizes. His green eyes flashed with happiness. Hunger gnawed at Jasper's gut. He would do anything to keep Abel smiling.

While chuckling like a naughty child, Abel pulled two matching silicone bracelets from the bag. He worked one of the thick, red bracelets onto Jasper's wrist before pulling the other on. "There. We match." Jasper's throat unexpectedly swelled. Before he could work out his emotions or respond, Abel plopped a pair of plastic sunglasses on Jasper's face. "I got you some candy too."

Jasper pushed the sunglasses up his nose, owning the ridiculous look. "Thanks babe. You ready to head out?"

With a bright smile stretching his lips, Abel accepted Jasper's hand. He didn't get in any hurry as he headed for the car. Jasper wasn't ready for his time with Abel to end, especially since he knew—after today—it would be a few days before he saw Abel again. His mood darkened as he drove. He wondered if Abel would let him keep him. As he parked in front of Abel's house, Jasper decided to just put it out there.

"I have to go to Vegas for a few days to tie up some loose ends. You should come with me."

Abel's expression went through a myriad of emotions before finally smoothing. "I'm not free to do that but thank you for the offer."

Jasper bit back a chuckle. Abel's response reminded him of a politician. His words could have meant anything. Not being free could be anything from having to work to being married. Jasper knew neither of those things were true. Still, he decided not to force things. "Can I see you when I get back?"

A sweet smile touched Abel's lips. "I'd like that."

With a nod, Jasper took Abel's hand and kissed the back. "Thank you for hanging out with me today. It was fun."

"It was. Thank you for inviting me." Abel grabbed the door handle, obviously ready to make his escape now that things were turning personal.

Jasper released Abel's hand and let him jump from the car. He understood Abel's turmoil. The moment Abel's feet hit the sidewalk; Jasper chose to rattle Abel a bit more. "By the way, I forgot to tell you, you look really sexy today."

Abel paused. After a second, he simply closed the door behind him, as of pretending he hadn't heard. An evil chuckle rose in Jasper's throat as he drove away. He couldn't wait to fuck with Abel's head a little more. Today had been fun. They would be together again soon.

·♥·♥·♥·♥·♥·

As Abel tried making his way inside, Griffin appeared from nowhere and linked his arm through Abel's. Abel flashed his brother a smile, hoping to hide his impatience to be alone. He already always felt like the worst brother. It had just been a strange day and Abel needed time to think.

"Hey, sweetie."

Griffin's eyes flashed with mischief. "Were you on a *date*?" The way Griffin said *date* was so scandalous.

"Maybe," Abel said, trying to sound cryptic before immediately breaking. "He's a professional boxer. We met at lunch yesterday. He's really great, Griff. I feel like a ridiculous teenager or something." He pressed his hand to his cheek, trying to cool his overheated face.

Griffin looked slightly confused, which was fair. It wasn't like Abel to gush over a man. "You just met yesterday?"

Abel nodded. "I know. It's weird. I swear it's like we've known each other forever."

With a shake of his head, Griffin kissed Abel's cheek. "As long as you're happy, that's all I care about."

Abel shrugged. "I mean, like I said, we just met. We'll see. You know me. I could still fuck things up."

"You're doing great." Griffin squeezed his arm one final time and released him. "I need to find my husband, but it's good to see you smile. Keep it up."

With a nod, Abel rushed up the stairs. With his head a bit of a mess, Abel headed for his room without looking right or left. As he hit the third floor, his steps slowed. He half expected to find a mask hanging from the door. His heart dropped a little when he found the knob empty again. Abel's emotions were all over the place. Sir was the man who had saved him. He was the person who made Abel's body burn. Sir was the stranger who would never show Abel his face. He would never take Abel to an arcade and play silly games with him. Abel was Sir's dark secret. The guy probably had a wife and three kids. Abel didn't even know his name. Sir had paid for Abel... like a whore, except Sir never let Abel touch him in return. Fuck. Abel was so confused.

Abel shoved his way into his room and dropped his bag of absurd prizes on the dresser. He didn't know why he was being ridiculous. Jasper was only a friend. Abel was picking everything apart like Jasper had given him any hope they would ever be anything more. His gaze dropped to the silicone bracelet he wore. It was such a cheap and childish thing, but they matched. Jasper probably took his off the moment Abel closed the car door. Abel hooked his thumb on the bracelet and started to peel it off. He stopped.

Maybe he wouldn't take it off just yet. No one had to know he clung to something hopeless. It had been a long time since he felt this alive. Abel couldn't let the feeling go.

With a growl, he headed for the bathroom. He would brush his teeth and take a shower. Maybe once he was clean, he would find some real food. He didn't know when Sir planned to visit him again, but Abel needed to make some everyday charges to his card or Sir would be furious. It was bad enough Abel hadn't gone to Jasper's fight or bought himself lunch today. He couldn't keep pushing Sir's patience.

It wasn't until Abel stood beneath a stream of hot water that he questioned himself. Maybe he was pushing Sir on purpose. Abel didn't know anymore. He hadn't felt this torn in a long time. On one hand, he had just met this great guy who might not want to be more than friends. On the other, Abel had this mystery savior who owned way too many of Abel's thoughts for no more than Abel knew about him. Maybe Abel kind of wanted to force Sir's hand. He didn't have to eat dinner tonight.

Once clean, Abel climbed from the shower with his head in the clouds. He went back and forth with himself. With a towel wrapped around his waist, Abel watched the sun dip lower in the sky. He didn't know what to do. A knock landed on his bedroom door. Abel's heart climbed into his throat. He should have gotten something to eat. Sir's punishment could be anything. Abel's hands shook as he opened the door.

Silas stood on the other side. He held out a black and red satin mask to Abel. "You have a guest."

Without a word, Abel took the mask from Silas and closed the door. All the inner debating no longer mattered. Sir was here. Abel moved to the chair and sat. He stared at the door. Something rebellious rose inside him. He didn't have to put on the mask. All he had to do was sit there. Sir would open the door and the game would end. Abel would know his benefactor's face. And Abel would likely be out on his ass with nowhere to go. He would be homeless and broke with zero prospects. The doorknob turned and Abel panicked. He quickly donned the mask before he was caught disobeying. His heart beat so fast and hard Abel could hear it pounding in his ears. That didn't stop him from hearing the fury in Sir's voice.

"Stand up."

Abel stood.

"Drop the towel."

Abel let his towel slide to the floor.

Sir crossed the room. His presence was so huge, Abel knew exactly where he stood without having to see him. "You disobeyed me."

After his debate about wearing the mask, Abel almost forgot about not attending the fight. It took him a second to catch up. "I tried, but I wasn't brave enough to go inside."

Sir took a step closer.

Abel braced to get hit, and he had no idea why. Sir had never slapped him. It was instinctual.

Instead, Sir's fingers traced Abel's jaw. "Did you decide you weren't brave enough to eat today either?"

For some reason, Abel suddenly didn't want to share Jasper with anyone. He dodged. "I was just getting ready to go find something."

Sir dropped his hand to Abel's waist. He swiped his palm from Abel's side to his hip. "I don't know if I can trust that. You're becoming defiant."

"I'm not." Too late Abel realized that was exactly what a defiant person would say.

In a flash, Sir had commandeered Abel's seat and Abel found himself facedown across Sir's knees. The first strike landed across his ass. Abel gasped at the impact he hadn't seen coming. The second one came before Abel processed the first.

Sir stroked Abel's ass. "Do you like your life with me?"

Abel didn't answer fast enough. His earlier thoughts about outing Sir rose to the surface and tied his tongue at exactly the wrong moment. A third slap stung his ass cheek. Abel gasped for air. He bit his tongue to keep from moaning as his dick hardened. When the fourth strike landed, Abel couldn't hold back any longer. A moan tore from his throat. His cock twitched. He couldn't think straight. His body was on fire. Abel wanted to get fucked. It had been so long. Sir's blow jobs were amazing, but Abel missed being stretched wide and pounded hard. He wanted bruises on his skin and teeth sinking into his flesh. God, he craved feeling alive.

Sir swiped his hand across Abel's ass cheek, stroking him. Then his fingers dug into Abel's crack, finding his hole. Abel bit his bottom lip hard enough to taste blood. He feared, if he begged, Sir would stop.

"Is this what you hoped to accomplish by defying me?" A finger found its way inside Abel's asshole. "Do you want this?"

"Yes." God help him. The confession ripped from Abel's chest. He needed more.

For a moment, Sir didn't move or respond. He simply held still with one finger in Abel's ass.

Abel held his breath.

A second finger joined the first. "Don't move." The gravelly words were all the warning Abel got before Sir spit on his asshole and went to work. He punched and massaged at Abel's prostate. Abel braced his hands on the floor and tried to stay still. His cock leaked pre-cum on Sir's legs while Sir fucked Abel's ass with his fingers. Abel squeezed his eyes closed while Sir pleasured him. The pressure grew until Abel thought he would snap. He needed more, but he knew he wouldn't get it. Then Sir pushed at exactly the right moment and Abel flew apart. He shook uncontrollably while Sir worked every spasm from Abel. Abel gasped for air, trying to cling to his sanity in the aftermath of Sir's destruction.

Sir softly stroked Abel's ass. "That's it, gorgeous. Take a breath. When I leave here, I expect you to get cleaned up, dressed, and go find something to eat. Your health means everything to me. I don't enjoy punishing you."

Abel fought the sudden urge to cry. He had two men taking care of him in different ways, yet he had no one. Sometimes, it felt like he was doomed to be this half person who never knew normalcy. Only once in his entire life had he been halfway adjusted, and that guy had married Abel's brother. Life felt pointless. Abel didn't know if he wanted it anymore. Maybe if he just held his breath, he would never start again. It was scary how badly he wanted to find out.

Chapter Four

♥

THREE DAYS WITHOUT A word from Jasper or Sir had Abel in a weird mood. Silas was having one of his parties and Abel's skin felt too tight. He never attended, but he always wondered if Sir was right downstairs. It wasn't like Abel could pick him from the crowd, but what if he was? What if Sir checked out the latest wares and searched for Abel's replacement? All while Abel sat right here only one or two floors away none the wiser. It was very possible Sir had six more men stashed away just like Abel. Maybe Sir never wanted his sexual favors reciprocated because he had a dozen other men on standby. It wouldn't surprise Abel. He wasn't special.

In the hallway window seat on the third floor, Abel sat mostly hidden behind the thick curtains. Anytime Silas had one of his secret parties—like the one where Sir had found Abel— Abel stayed out of sight. The general party setting was too much for Abel's mental health. Already Abel's skin crawled with a need to wreck his sobriety. He distracted himself by focusing on small things. Abel inspected each face as they passed through the gate, wondering which one belonged to Sir.

There was a guy on the front lawn dressed as a peacock. He distracted Abel as he literally flashed his feathers, preening for a mate. Abel wanted to be embarrassed for him, but Abel couldn't judge. The only one of these parties he had attended, Abel had been high to the edge of death. Silas had locked him in a cage and offered him to anyone willing to save him. As terrible as that sounded, Abel had asked Silas to do it. He had needed help. Desperation bred strange bedfellows. Abel needed to hand his life over to someone else's control or go ahead and die. He had chosen life. Most people wouldn't understand this strange existence he lived now. Abel was literally fighting to stay alive. Sir kept him alive.

Abel turned his face away from the window. He didn't know the peacock's story. Maybe he was just trying to make it through the night too. With nothing else to hold his attention, Abel stared down the hall. His window seat was at one end and a lone door sat at the other. The bedrooms of Silas' projects—Abel included—were on each side of the hallway in between. In front of the lone doorway at the end of the hall stood a man. Abel only knew the dark-haired, wide-shouldered guy because of his failed engagement to Andrew.

Andrew managed Silas's strip club, Assets. The man at the end of the hall, guarded the door of Assets with his scarily large size. Abel was fairly certain his name was Kage. Since it wasn't Abel's house, outside of his bedroom, Abel stuck to the normal open areas: hallways, the kitchen, etc. He had never paid much attention to the door Kage guarded now. Abel assumed it was someone's bedroom and therefore none of his concern. In his boredom and thanks to it having a guard, Abel's mind pounced on the topic to stay sane. Now that he thought about it, every other door had a fancy golden number. Griffin and Andrew currently lived in number one. Abel was across the hall in number two. The rest of the rooms were empty as far as Abel knew. He saw no one come or go. But the door Kage guarded had no number. It was odd.

As he looked on, Kage went from leaning casually against the door to widening his stance. He went on alert, as if prepared to defend his secret door. Abel's gaze shot to the mouth of the nearby staircase. A tall man with wide shoulders and light brown hair appeared at the top of the stairs. He didn't spare Kage a glance as he turned Abel's way. It was Jasper, except it didn't look like the laughing man who commandeered Abel's table at that first lunch. This was the Jasper that stepped into the ring. Abel knew that without having to see him fight.

Jasper wore all black. His suit had a slight sheen to it like the material was fine and cost a fortune, but everything about it was solid black. His coat, vest, tie, shirt, pants, belt, and shoes. None it had any color, but the material molded to Jasper's skin perfectly. He looked expensive and Abel's lips parted on a pant at the severity of his expression and outfit. He liked Jasper's smile and the way he laughed. This was different. This Jasper would bend Abel to his will. Goddamn. He was sexy. That didn't explain why he was here. Before Abel could call out to him, Jasper pulled something from his pocket. His sleeve rose a hair and Abel caught sight of the red silicone bracelet. A smile pulled at the corners of Abel's mouth. Happiness swelled in his chest. With his head down, staring at whatever he held, Jasper stopped outside Abel's bedroom door. Abel nearly bounced from his seat.

"Jasper."

Jasper's head shot up at the sound of his name. His gaze found Abel's hiding spot. He put whatever he held back in his pocket. A smile exploded across his face, bringing back the Jasper Abel knew. He headed Abel's way. "Hey. I didn't see you hiding back there."

Abel held open the curtain, inviting Jasper into his secret spot. He saw Kage relax his stance and return to ignoring them. No doubt Kage was paid well to see nothing and protect whatever. Abel appreciated it now. He didn't want witnesses for how happy he was to see Jasper.

"I got bored, so I was people watching. How are you here? I thought you didn't do parties."

Jasper opened his lapel enough to show a cream-colored invitation in his inside coat pocket. Abel recognized it immediately as the ones Silas always sent out for these exclusive parties. "I got this tonight when I got home. It said I should come see you."

Abel's lips parted in surprise. Why would Silas do that... unless Sir was losing interest. Abel didn't know how to feel.

If Jasper noticed Abel's inner turmoil, he didn't show it. He kept chatting happily as he sat near Abel's feet on the window seat. "I couldn't find you when I first got here, so I asked around. Finally, some dude in a pink bunny costume said you were up here in room two."

At the mention of a pink bunny, an unwanted wave of jealousy hit Abel. He had already lost one man to falling in love with his little brother. "That's my brother, Griffin." He watched Jasper for even the tiniest reaction.

Jasper looked thoughtful. "Come to think of it, he did kind of look like you."

Defeat washed over Abel. "Yep. He's the hot one."

Jasper curled his nose, looking adorable to Abel. "He's a child."

Abel snorted. "I assure you, he's not."

"He is to me," Jasper said, sounding horrified. "I'm old enough to be his dad."

Despite his guilt over his jealousy, a laugh sneaked out. "No, you're not."

Jasper's expression didn't lose an ounce of happiness. "If you knew how young I was when I started fucking everyone who would let me, you'd see I'm right. He's way too young for me." Jasper's expression turned heated. His gaze swept down Abel's body. "Not to mention, I am completely enamored with someone else."

"What's his name?"

A bright smile lit Jasper's face. He snagged the edge of the curtain and pulled it closed, completely hiding them from sight. His eyes danced with laughter, but—oddly—Abel didn't think he was amused. In fact, he thought Jasper was dangerous. His breath caught in the back of his throat. For a second, Abel considered running. Then Jasper grabbed him by the throat and his mouth slammed down onto Abel's. There was no air. Only lust existed. Abel realized he had never been kissed. Not really. Not like this. This was carnal. This was a kiss by a man who liked to use his mouth to bring fantasies to life. Abel wanted more.

He twisted Jasper's lapels between his hands, dragging him closer. Until that moment, Abel hadn't realized he had reached for Jasper. He tugged, tearing at Jasper's clothes like they weren't barely hidden from sight. The way Jasper held him in place by his neck and the way he devastated Abel's mouth had Abel ready to fuck. No sugar coating anything. He wanted teeth, nails, and violence.

Jasper pulled away but didn't release Abel's throat. His eyes flashed with something too dark for Abel to explain, but he knew he wasn't in control. Jasper eyed Abel's mouth for a moment. When he spoke, his voice sounded deeper than usual. "Make no mistake, you are mine. I will fuck you right here where anyone outside who looks up can watch. So you have two choices. I can peel your pants off right now, take what I want, and then you can try to pretend I was never here. Or you can admit defeat and we can go to bed where you can get fucked the way you deserve. Either way, I will be inside you tonight, and you will still be mine in the morning."

Abel couldn't breathe. He had never been so aroused. He couldn't function. His body wasn't his any longer.

"Tick tock, Abel. I'm not known for my patience."

Abel blinked. There was something about Jasper's voice. Something familiar. It was the deep way he said Abel's name. With his mind coated in lust, the answer was just out of reach.

"Time's up."

Abel scrambled to his feet, scared Jasper would leave, even though Jasper had made it clear he wouldn't. "We'll go to bed."

"Good choice."

With his decision made, Abel headed for his bedroom door. His insides shook and he tried not to make eye contact with Kage since he knew he had to look as disheveled as he felt. As Abel led Jasper inside his room, Jasper invaded Abel's space. He kissed the side of Abel's neck. "I missed you while I was gone."

Abel's eyes fell closed at the claim. Damn. He didn't know if Jasper meant it, but Abel loved hearing it. Honestly, he hadn't completely believed Jasper wanted to be more than friends until that kiss. Now, he couldn't cool down. Unfortunately, he was also a fucked-up mess.

The moment Jasper closed the door behind them, Abel turned and practically jumped away, putting space between them. He walked backward, babbling in his nervousness. "You look really amazing. This suit... wow. There's no doubt it was tailored to fit."

Jasper's expression never softened. "Strip." As Jasper made the demand, he unbuttoned his jacket.

Abel swallowed. His hands shook as he lifted his shirt and peeled it off. While Abel had never lacked in self-esteem, he wasn't the person he used to be. Abel used to walk into a club, pick the hottest guy there, and take him down. Then Abel had woken up a junkie one day. He didn't feel the same on the inside any longer.

As if Jasper read his mind, he tossed his coat aside and closed the distance between them. Jasper cupped Abel's face between his hands. "Don't lose that beautiful bravery now." He claimed Abel's mouth. Jasper kept their kiss sweet.

Something inside Abel melted. His hands found Jasper's vest. He unbuttoned the piece and pushed it down Jasper's hard shoulders. His heart sped. Jasper's body felt amazing beneath his palms. He fought the urge to shape every perfect line. Abel knew it was Jasper's job to stay in shape, but damn. Jasper was like marble. Abel couldn't get enough of Jasper's kiss. It was as if the guy loved to use his tongue and it showed. Abel kept getting distracted while peeling away the layers of Jasper's suit. The loving way Jasper kissed him fed Abel's courage. He felt powerful in a way he hadn't in years. Abel tugged at Jasper's clothing without an ounce of shame. Tomorrow, he could think about the consequences. In the morning, he would have to think about Sir.

Jasper kissed a path to Abel's neck, sending goosebumps skirting down Abel's skin. He was so turned on, he could barely breathe. Everything from Jasper's lips to his delicious scent appealed to Abel. Abel couldn't get him naked fast enough. As Abel pushed Jasper's pants down his hips, something hit the floor. Abel automatically dropped his gaze. His heart stopped. His lungs froze. A red and black mask along with a keyring that matched Abel's rested next to Abel's foot. Abel shoved, obviously catching Jasper off guard since he let it happen. Abel stared at the items on the floor. It was like there was no air. No matter how hard or fast Abel breathed, no oxygen reached his brain. Only one other key existed besides his: Sir's.

Jasper's gaze moved from Abel to the floor and back again. "Abel, I—"

Abel bolted. He didn't wait to hear anything Jasper had to say. His feet couldn't move fast enough. It couldn't be true. He needed space. Abel had to think. Surely Jasper wouldn't trick him like that. He thought they were friends. As Abel hit the hallway, he glanced in every direction, looking for an escape. His feet and chest were bare. He had no money or phone. There was a party raging below and Abel's brain wouldn't work. The door opened at the end of the hallway, hitting Kage in the back. Kage quickly stuck his head inside. After a second, his gaze landed on Abel. He waved for Abel to come. Abel raced in Kage's direction, needing any help he could get. Kage pushed him inside the room and closed the door.

With his heart pumping too fast to be useful, it took Abel a second to get his bearings. He stood at the foot of a staircase, and he wasn't alone. A tiny guy covered in tattoos stood inches away. He took Abel's hand and led him to the stairs before pulling him down to sit next to him on the step. Once they were sitting hip to hip, he leaned into Abel's side and held his phone out for Abel to see. Abel's gaze moved from the man's perfect features to the screen. He realized he stared at the hallway outside the door. It was a security feed. As they looked on, Jasper shot from Abel's room half dressed. He looked furious in a way that scared Abel. He tore open the curtains at the window seat. Finding it empty, he headed Kage's way.

"Where did he go?"

Kage looked completely unfazed as he motioned toward the stairs. With a scowl, Jasper hit the stairs running. Abel took a breath and then another. Each one sounded ragged as hell. He looked his savior's way. The bright phone screen highlighted his features.

"What's your name?"

"Benji." His eyes never wavered from the screen of his phone as he answered.

Abel couldn't look away from him. As God was his witness, Abel had never seen anyone more beautiful. He had a long, ragged scar above his ear that started at his temple and ended near the base of Benji's head. It did nothing to deter from the man's beauty.

After a moment, Benji's phone went dark, and he looked Abel's way. "I think you're safe now."

His eyes were the lightest gray Abel had ever seen. He was mesmerizing. "Thank you."

Benji nodded. "You were lucky. I was watching the cameras. You don't have to cry. I can take care of you."

Until Benji pointed it out, Abel didn't realize tears streamed unchecked down his face. Once he noticed, the tears came harder. He sniffed. "I'm sorry." He sucked in a ragged breath. "I can't seem to stop."

"You don't have to be sorry. I cry all the time."

He was so sweet. Abel wished he could think straight. Everything hurt. He could barely breathe.

The door flew open, sending Abel's heart racing into his throat. Silas stood in the doorway, holding the door open and looking half insane—like he had raced up the stairs and feared the worst. His chest heaved as he looked between them. Obviously realizing everything was fine, he audibly sucked in a breath and tried composing himself.

Benji rubbed Abel's back. "It's okay. Daddy's here."

Silas's hands shook as he pulled some folded bills from his pocket and passed them Kage's way. "Thank you for your help and for letting me know there was a problem. You can go." He barely spared Abel a glance. "Jasper is gone. You're safe to go back to your room."

In his confusion and shock, Abel stood and quietly accepted his dismissal. It wasn't until he stood in the hallway, staring at a closed door, that reality hit him. Everyone in his life had known. Abel had been blissfully building a friendship with the man who had been sucking his dick for several months. Abel bent at the waist and sucked air. Everyone knew, except Abel. At one point in time, everyone in his life had been sent to inform Abel when he had a guest and deliver his mask on Jasper's behalf. Fuck. Abel really couldn't breathe. He couldn't think. It was possible things weren't as bad as they seemed. But, at the moment, he couldn't tell. He was in information overload. Abel was on the verge of collapse. He was the closest he had been since leaving rehab to calling his dealer.

A warm palm landed on his shoulder and squeezed. Abel's head shot up. He was ready to strike. It was Kage.

"Let's find you a shirt and some shoes. You probably shouldn't stay here tonight. That guy looked pretty dangerous. I imagine it won't take him long before he comes back."

With a nod, Abel straightened and let Kage take over his life. It seemed the sanest thing to do since Abel obviously had no business being in control.

·♥·♥·♥·♥·♥·

Crazed didn't begin to describe Jasper's mood. Two minutes after flying down the stairs in search of Abel, Silas had yelled for everyone to get out. He didn't know if Abel had gone straight for Silas and begged to be hidden. Jasper knew nothing except he had fucked up.

He had shown up jet-lagged from rushing to get home to Abel. His head hadn't been on straight. The invitation to Silas's party had arrived and Jasper had shoved a mask and Abel's key in his pocket with no real plan in mind. He had shown up at Silas's and gone upstairs with his heart split in two. Part of him wanted to let himself into Abel's room and reveal himself. Another part of him thought to knock on the door and just be Abel's friend. The last thing he had expected was Abel to be in the hallway. That had taken away his time to think. He hadn't been able to break his dark mood before approaching Abel.

Now everything was fucked. Jasper dug his phone out and called the phone he had given Abel when he first rescued him. His call went straight to voicemail twice. The third time, the call connected, but no one spoke. That was fine. Jasper only needed Abel to listen.

"Don't hang up. Come outside. Let me explain."

"I just needed to hear your voice to prove I'm not crazy. You really are Sir."

Jasper pushed through his desperation. "I am, but listen."

"This is the last call I'll take from you," Abel said, interrupting him and sounding dead. "I'm leaving everything you bought me behind. Feel free to collect it after I'm gone."

"After you're gone. What?" The call disconnected, leaving Jasper enraged.

He glanced toward the front gate. Two private security guards hired for the party were still stationed outside, keeping people out. There was no way for Jasper to sneak back inside. He looked up and tried to see Abel's window from the street. It was no use. Silas's house was like a fortress. Jasper would know. He had once lived there too. Any hope of seeing Abel was dead. Jasper didn't know where to go from here.

Chapter Five

♥

AFTER ONLY A HANDFUL of words exchanged between them, Abel fell face first across Kage's couch and didn't move. He managed a fitful night of sleep before giving up around sunrise. Kage came through the living room about eight and motioned toward the door.

"Want to go for a run with me?"

Abel shook his head and Kage left without him. Once he was alone, Abel eyed his surroundings. His shock had been too thick for him to check out the place sooner. Kage's house was nice. Oddly nice. It was small but pretty.

The wood floors were beautiful—like care had gone into them. Abel stood and gave himself a tour. The kitchen had a small wooden table with two chairs on one end. On the other, the walls were covered in double cabinets that went all the way to the ceiling. The upper cabinets were decorated glass while bottom cabinets were white. Abel fought the urge to run his hand across the expensive-looking marble countertops. It was genuinely gorgeous. Abel's curiosity spiked. He headed down the hall.

The first door Abel came to was a bathroom. He dipped inside and took advantage of finding a place to pee. Abel grabbed his overnight bag and lingered, washing his face and brushing his teeth. Afterward, he went back to exploring. The room across from the bathroom was a home gym.

Abel wasn't surprised. Kage was solid as hell. He obviously spent a lot of time on his body somewhere. There was one more door at the end of the hall. Abel assumed it was Kage's bedroom. The room was dark despite the bright sun pouring through the rest of the windows in the house. Abel lingered outside the door and sneaked a quick peek inside before quickly retreating. He didn't want to be nosy, but he was curious about Kage. This was a nice place for a bouncer slash door guard. The house wasn't huge, but it couldn't be cheap either.

Abel headed back to the living room before he got caught snooping. As he sank into the plush leather couch, the front door opened. Kage stepped inside covered in sweat and carrying a paper bag. He smiled when his gaze landed on Abel.

He shook the bag at Abel. "I run past a beignet shop every morning. For you, I let temptation win today." He dropped the bag on the coffee table before peeling off his shirt. He used the material to wipe the sweat from his brow while Abel tried not to swallow his tongue. Even in his screwed-up state, Abel recognized Kage was a prize. Men probably crawled over each other kicking and punching to get to Kage. Abel tried to look everywhere but at the freshly bared mile of hard chest.

"It smells good." He didn't know if he meant the food or Kage's body. Goddamn. Life wasn't fair. Some men were clearly God's favorite.

Kage nodded as he peeled open the sticker that held the bag closed.

"They're good at packing to-go orders. There's coffee in here too. It didn't spill at all during my jog."

"Mhmm. I thought I smelled coffee. You're amazing."

Kage's eyes flashed with humor as he set a paper coffee cup in front of Abel. "You're too easy to impress."

"I'm easy in every way." Abel blinked as the words left his lips. He had said nothing the least bit flirtatious in ages. The words had popped from his lips without thought.

The sexy chuckle that rumbled from Kage made Abel's embarrassment worthwhile. Kage sat on the floor with his back against the couch and went to work doctoring his coffee. Abel slid to the floor beside him. Together, they ate breakfast in silence.

Abel chewed while lost in thought. He couldn't stay with Kage forever. Kage wouldn't want to support him. Abel needed a job and a plan.

"I really have no fucking clue where to start," Abel said aloud before he realized Kage couldn't read his mind. He clarified so Kage wouldn't think he was a moron. "I guess I need to find a job. Damn."

Kage nodded. "You can't go back to Silas's place."

Abel's shoulders fell at Kage confirming his worst fears. "It looks like I'm homeless... again." He looked Kage's way. "What's wrong with me? I know you're not my psychiatrist, but really. Why are people like me born? I serve no real purpose. I don't have a destiny or whatever. My life is a joke."

Kage held his coffee cup to his lips, looking thoughtful before setting the cup away without taking a sip. "I don't know about destiny or anything like that, but I'm glad you exist, and I think it's for a reason. You saved me last night."

Before he could stop it from happening, Abel pulled a disbelieving face. "Okay."

A sad smile touched Kage's lips as he looked Abel's way. "You did. Yesterday was the anniversary of my husband's death. We built this house together." He motioned absently at their surroundings. "I've been saving all the extra money Silas has been paying me on the side. Last night, I'd planned to do one final job for Silas and then burn this place to ground before disappearing. My bags are still in the car."

"Why would you want to do that? This place is beautiful."

"It's a shrine of lies." There was a dead note to Kage's voice that Abel recognized too well. "There's a bartender job open at Assets," Kage said, changing the subject. "Considering the manager is your brother-in-law, I'm sure all you have to do is ask, and he'd hire you. You'd be looking at naked ass all night and serving entitled pricks, but the money is good. You can stay with me until you're on your feet."

The last thing Abel wanted was to ask Andrew for a job, but times were tough. Also, maybe he needed to stay with Kage for a bit. It sounded like they needed each other. No one had needed him in a long time. It was time for a fresh start.

·❤·❤·❤·❤·❤·

All Jasper did was pace the floor. He saw every second tick by on the clock. His nerves twitched like they hadn't in years. The only thing that soothed him was being with Abel. Jasper had ruined any chance of that. He didn't know how to fix it. Jasper had decided not to collect Abel's things in hopes

Abel went home. He called Abel's phone nonstop, praying Abel came back. Each time, his call went to voicemail. He couldn't stop picturing Abel strung out in a crack house or dead in an alleyway.

When a banging started on his front door, Jasper raced to answer, uncaring if he looked as desperate as he felt. He was losing his goddamn mind not knowing where Abel was. Jasper jerked open the door. Outrage stared back at him.

"What did you do to my brother?"

Jasper eyed the younger version of Abel. His eyes flashed with innocent rage—like an angry puppy. "Hello, Griffin."

Griffin huffed and stamped his foot. "Don't 'hello Griffin' me. What did you do to my brother?"

Jasper waved Griffin inside. He supposed there should be some comeuppance for mishandling the situation. Plus, he really needed to explain himself to someone. The desperation to confess ate at the lining of his stomach. Jasper spoke over his shoulder as he led Griffin to the couch.

"I'm a recovering alcoholic. During the worst of it, I lost everything." Jasper sat and waited for Griffin to do the same.

Instead, Griffin hovered over him, looking ready to fight. "What does that have to do with Abel?"

Jasper patted the spot beside him, refusing to say more until Griffin sat.

With a huff, Griffin dropped onto the couch. "Go on."

The obnoxiousness in Griffin's tone almost made Jasper smile. Unfortunately, he had lost that ability since he lost Abel.

"It has everything to do with Abel," Jasper said, picking up where he left off. "I ruined my career. Lost my house and ended up homeless. Silas took me in and got me sober. He saved me. Because of him, I'm the US champ and I have more than most people can dream of having. But nothing is free with Silas. He calls in his favors." Jasper held Griffin's stare as he spoke, ensuring Griffin understood Silas would likely expect something of him someday. "Nine months ago, he called and asked me to take a look at one of his pets. I honestly thought I would simply humor him. Then I got there, and I saw Abel. It was like looking into a mirror and seeing my past self. I couldn't leave him like that."

Griffin made an impatient gesture. "Skip to the part where you broke him."

A sad smile tugged at Jasper's lips. "I thought I wouldn't get attached if he didn't touch me while I fixed him the same way Silas fixed me."

Griffin's chest expanded as he took a deep breath. Then his eyes fell closed. When they opened again, Griffin looked defeated. "I saw you bring him home the other day. Right away, I realized he didn't know you were his benefactor. I didn't out you and now he thinks we all betrayed him." A desperate and humorless bark of laughter burst from Griffin. He covered his mouth and tears filled his eyes. Griffin blinked them away, but when he spoke, his voice broke. "This might really be how I lose my brother. How dumb is that? I married his ex-fiancé." Griffin shook his head. "He never once shamed or blamed me for that. But this... I might not come back from this. All because I protected you."

"I won't let that happen." The words burst from Jasper with all the anger and passion in his heart. He wouldn't allow Abel to shut out the people keeping him alive. Then Jasper remembered he didn't know how to find him. "I should've put a tracker in his shoe or something. Fuck."

Griffin chewed the side of his nail while he watched Jasper flounder. After a moment, he dropped his hand and swiped his palms on his thighs. "I know where he is. Well, I know where he'll be tonight."

Jasper's muscles tensed. He fought the urge to shake the info from Griffin. "Go on."

"You have to swear to me you won't make things worse. I can't lose my brother."

All Jasper needed was five minutes alone with Abel. Abel would comply. "I swear."

Griffin nodded. Jasper felt Abel move within his grasp. Abel belonged to him. He had sworn to behave for Jasper. Abel would come back to him. If not, he would be sorry.

Chapter Six

♥

"YOU WON'T MAKE IT through the night."

Abel refused to fidget or buckle under Andrew's claim. He needed a job. They were family now. Andrew had to help him. If not, Abel might end up dead. No dramatics. He wasn't strong like other people. "I can serve drinks to a bunch of drunk perverts. It can't be hard." Abel tried to look as confident as anyone could while wearing no shirt and a bowtie. He really wished Andrew had voiced his objections before Abel donned the dumbass half uniform.

Andrew shook his head. "It's not that. Jasper will show up to get you before the end of night. There's no way he'll tolerate you working here."

Abel's shoulders squared. He clasped his hands behind his back to hide the way they shook. Abel couldn't outright prove Andrew had known about Jasper's trickery. If so, he wouldn't be here. Then again, Andrew owed him a kick in the balls, so whatever. Abel needed the money. "It doesn't matter if he shows. I don't belong to him. It's time for me to find my footing."

Andrew eyed Abel in silence in a way only Andrew could. Abel often wondered how he had ever gotten away with cheating on Andrew. He swore Andrew had the magic ability to see right through his bullshit.

Andrew's stare always made Abel feel exposed. That was probably why Abel had been so scared of marrying him.

After a moment, Andrew sighed and sat forward. He leaned his elbows on his desk. A sad smile touched his lips. "I'll never forget when Silas told me he had chosen me for Griffin." Abel didn't want to hear this, but it didn't stop Andrew. "At the time, it annoyed me," Andrew said with a chuckle. "I'm the one who chose Griffin. In fact, it was important to me that everyone understood I chose him over you. The thing is, though, I think Silas did choose me." Andrew made a dismissive motion, as if he knew he sounded crazy, but he didn't want Abel to stop him. "I know how it sounds, but it's almost like he knew. Like he could see the future. When Griffin showed up here looking for a job, I was hellbent against it. Silas overruled me and I swear he looked at me and saw my heart. He knew something I didn't. Then he stirred my jealousy by always trying to take Griffin away. Griffin says they spent countless nights, staying up all night, where Silas basically counseled him to good mental health... for me. He did it because he knew I needed that stability. As much as I have never wanted to think of Silas as anything more than a bored, rich guy who collects pretty things, I think he knows. If he paired you with Jasper, that's where you should be. That's who you should be with right now. Don't ask me how, but some fucking how, Silas knows. You won't make it through the night."

Abel took a steadying breath, trying to pull air past the lump in his throat. He barely held back the angry tears that burned the backs of his eyes. "I don't know what Silas knew in advance. But I know what he knew while it was happening, and I can't live with that. I can't live with everyone watching me get played for a fool and staying quiet. If the end goal was to keep me clean, their plan failed miserably because I'm barely hanging on. I need this job. I swear I'll find something else as quickly as possible so I'm not in your face all the time. Trust me, I know you hate the sight of me. This is temporary, but I need your help right now."

Andrew blew out a tired-sounding sigh. "I don't hate the sight of you. You're welcome to work here for as long as you need. We're family now. No matter our past, you didn't deserve what Jasper did. He should've been straight with you."

Abel's teeth protested the pressure of his locked jaw. It took all of Abel's strength not to cry. Life had humbled him a lot. In fact, he couldn't recall a time when life had been fair. He had been raised by abusive parents, then made every bad decision known to man while trying to survive the damage. Abel could and would stand shirtless behind a bar, smile, flirt, and fetch drinks. He would survive this.

"Thank you."

With a sharp nod, Andrew stood. "Let's get you started."

Abel released his pent-up breath and tried relaxing his shoulders. With a fake smile plastered on his lips, he followed Andrew from the office and onto the crowded main floor. Abel had survived worse. He would make it through this.

· ♥ · ♥ · ♥ · ♥ · ♥ ·

Assets was a nondescript building in a long line of nondescript buildings in the heart of the French Quarter. Despite its unimaginative outer appearance, inside was an exclusive strip club meant only for the rich and well-connected. No one else could afford the drinks or the dancers inside. Since Jasper didn't pay their obnoxiously high monthly membership fee, he was more than a little surprised to find his name on the list of guests for the evening. He supposed that was Griffin's doing, but Jasper had been prepared to pay any price to get inside.

As he stepped through the door of the brick building, the smell of alcohol slapped him in the face. Jasper tried taking slow breaths to keep from losing his mind. Flashbacks of nights he barely remembered washed over him. He wanted to fuck up his life.

A hand slid across his chest. "Hi. Would you like some company?"

Jasper looked over and met the empty stare of a guy half his age. "No. Thank you." With a shrug, the thong-clad guy moved on to his next target. Jasper had nothing against anyone doing what they had to do to survive. He simply wasn't here for that. Jasper had a target.

His gaze skimmed the room. A large guy with cold blue eyes and dark hair stepped into his path, blocking Jasper's way. "Are you here to start shit?"

Jasper eyed the guy's too tight shirt and gathered he was one of the bouncers. He looked a bit familiar, but Jasper couldn't place him. "I'm sure you'll let me know if I am."

A cruel smile stretched the guy's lips, as if he relished the idea of Jasper stepping out of line.

"Kage."

At the yell, the guy's gaze moved from Jasper toward the new arrival. Jasper glanced over his shoulder to find Abel's brother-in-law waiting for his guard dog to obey.

With a final sneer from Kage, he walked away, leaving Jasper to his hunt. Jasper went back to searching for Abel. He swore the crowd parted at the perfect moment. There he was, opening beers and passing them along like he had been there for years. His smile was brittle and fake. Jasper could see the slight hysteria in Abel's expression and the light dying in his eyes. Griffin was right to fear losing his brother. Abel barely held on.

Their gazes met. For a split second, Jasper saw Abel's relief. But then it died, as if the memory of Jasper's betrayal rose to the surface, killing everything good. Jasper's feet moved. He needed to get Abel out of this place. The scent of liquor and the sick feeling in Jasper's gut had Jasper ready to toss years of sobriety.

Andrew stepped into his path. "I put you on the guest list for Griffin's sake."

Jasper barely spared Andrew a glance. "Thanks." He tried stepping around Andrew, but the guy stepped back into his path.

"That doesn't mean I'll let you cause a scene in my club or hurt my family."

A growl rose in Jasper's throat. He swallowed it. Jasper doubted he would have much chance of winning Abel back tonight if he was in jail for assault. "I'm just here to collect my property."

A line appeared between Andrew's eyebrows. "Abel isn't property. He's a real person with thoughts and feelings.

Feelings you completely stomped, I might add."

Jasper's temper hit the roof. He wasn't known for his patience or his kindness. Jasper was known for his fists. He got the impression a few people needed reminding of that. Abel hadn't made him soft. He was soft for Abel. Everyone else was in the way. "Abel has an agreement with me. That agreement keeps him clean and off the streets. One way or the other, he's leaving here with me. If you truly want what's best for him, get the hell out of my way."

With a dip of his chin, Andrew stepped aside, but it was too late. Between the alcohol calling his name, everyone trying to stop him from getting to Abel, and Abel running away in the first place, Jasper was done playing. It was time for Abel to get back on track.

·♥·♥·♥·♥·♥·

Abel couldn't breathe. Jasper was really there. He looked hard and sexy. Abel wanted to bend to his will and that stiffened Abel's spine. Jasper was a liar. Abel shouldn't want him. He wouldn't want him. It was time for Abel to make better decisions. He needed to learn to be a functioning adult. If everyone else could do it, he could too.

Fuck. Jasper really looked hot. Even in jeans and a t-shirt, it was obvious he was expensive—like goddamn fine wine. Shit. Abel had to look away. He couldn't do this to himself. Jasper wasn't good for him.

Before Abel could find a place to hide, Jasper appeared at the edge of the bar. "Get your stuff. We're leaving."

A snort escaped Abel before he could stop it from happening. "Did you really think you would show up and I would drop everything at your command? No. Now, do you want a drink or what? Oh. Wait. You're an alcoholic... Supposedly." Abel had no idea what was the truth and what were lies.

Jasper's hard expression never wavered. Abel realized this was the real Jasper. Maybe the playful guy he had met at that first lunch existed somewhere inside Jasper, or maybe he didn't. Either way, this version was the true Jasper.

He didn't buckle under Abel's anger. "I never lied to you. Now get your things. Neither of us should be here."

Abel pushed away from the bar. "Stay or go. I don't care, but this is my job. I can't leave."

Jasper's face somehow got even harder. "Yes. You can. Let's go."

Despite his best efforts, Abel's pain rose to the surface and showed in his voice. "You should go. I have to work."

A growl escaped Jasper, sending chills down Abel's spine. "I'd planned to tell you who I was that night. Things got heated and then nothing mattered but finally having you the way I always pictured. I never intended to... ugh. Please just leave with me. I can't think with the smell of liquor hitting me from every direction."

"You should go." Abel would keep repeating himself as many times as it took. As angry as he was with Jasper, he didn't want him exposed to this much temptation. Alcohol had never been Abel's vice. He couldn't imagine being forced to stand in the middle of a room filled with people strung out. Abel wouldn't make it.

The muscles in Jasper's jaw flexed. "Not without having my say. Tell me I didn't matter, and I'll go. Tell me you couldn't feel that we were connected, even though you hadn't seen my face."

Abel felt sick. His chest hurt. He couldn't say what Jasper needed to hear to leave.

"This place isn't you. If you stay here, you'll eventually go back to who you were before I rescued you. If you can't leave with me, then go back to Silas. Pretend you don't know it's me. Let the people who love you take care of you."

At the mention of love, something inside Abel broke. His hand slammed down on the bar, rattling bottles and glasses, and turning heads their way. Abel spoke through clenched teeth. "No. Maybe I don't know much about love, but I know it doesn't lie. Everyone lied to me about you. Everyone knew your face but me."

"Leave with me."

"No."

Jasper opened his mouth as if to argue. Kage appeared at his back. "No is a complete sentence. Let's normalize that. It's time for you to leave."

As Abel looked on, Jasper became the hardened man who made money with his fists. He turned cold eyes Kage's way. "Back up, boy. You don't want to pick this fight."

Kage's eyes flashed with malicious intent. "Oh, but I do."

Jasper chuckled. It was an evil sound. "You don't know who you're fucking with."

A wicked smile stretched Kage's lips. "I definitely do, but you're obviously under the impression I plan to fight fair. You can leave with your life or without it, but either way, you're leaving."

"Please go." Even though Abel spoke the words quietly, Jasper cocked his head Abel's way, as if he heard. With a nod, he held his hands up in surrender and headed for the door.

"Come to this end of the bar, sweetie. I'll treat you right."

Abel's eyes fell closed at the taunt. Jasper was right. Abel didn't belong here. If he stayed, he would become his old self within a month. In a burst of helpless rage, Abel jumped the bar and went after Jasper. His fury built as the distance closed between them. His choices shouldn't be between lies and the gutter. Life wasn't supposed to be like this. Before he could stop himself, Abel shoved Jasper from behind, putting all his force into the motion.

Jasper spun, poised to strike his attacker. He immediately softened when his gaze landed on Abel.

Abel didn't let Jasper's unwillingness to fight him cool his temper. "You owe me more than demands. I did everything you asked. I exposed every weakness and desire for you. You couldn't even show me your face. Why would you pretend to be someone else? You could've just unmasked me. Why did you do it?" Even Abel heard the hurt and pleading in his voice. He didn't care. Jasper needed to see he had broken Abel.

"Leave with me and I'll tell you anything you want to know."

Abel held back tears as he shook his head. "Tell me now or don't speak to me again."

Jasper took a step forward so fast, Abel didn't have time to react. Barely an inch separated them. Jasper was close enough to kiss. Abel had never wanted anything more. Jasper held Abel's gaze and Abel knew whatever Jasper said next would be the purest truth. Jasper didn't disappoint. "Because I needed you to fall in love with me for me. I didn't want to rip off your mask and see Stockholm syndrome or Nightingale effect staring back at me."

Oddly, Abel didn't know which term best suited their relationship either. Jasper was both his captor and his savior.

Unfortunately, Jasper didn't stop there. He stroked Abel's cheek with the back of his knuckles. "I wanted you to love me the way I love you."

Abel took a step back. The move was more from shock than anything. The truth was in Jasper's eyes, though. He meant every word he spoke. A stuttered breath escaped Abel. "I'll go to Silas." The words were out there before Abel realized what he had done. He couldn't fucking breathe. Blindly, Abel turned away and pushed his way through the crowd. Someone said his name, but Abel didn't turn. His feet didn't stop moving until he was outside the back door and the night air filled his lungs. Abel held his side and sucked air. Why did he always have to be so damn weak? He just wanted to be strong like everyone else. Abel didn't want to need someone to make the hard decisions. The thing was, though, this was him. He was weak. Abel needed someone strong to make the hard decisions because he would always make the wrong ones. No one had given him the tools to be a functioning adult. He had two settings: submissive and self-destruct. Fighting his nature broke him.

A solid weight slammed against Abel's back. "Fuck this bullshit. I don't have what it takes to ask permission." Those growled words were all the warning Abel got before he found himself hanging over Jasper's shoulder. Abel hid his face against Jasper's back so no one would see his relief. Some people weren't meant to have independence. Abel was one of them.

Chapter Seven

♥

"YOU HAVE REAL FURNITURE."

These were the first words Abel had spoken to him since Jasper had carried him from the club. Even the car ride had been silent. Jasper was more relieved than he could say. The broken expression Abel had been wearing since running away from him at Assets was crushing the life from Jasper. "Yeah. You have a comfortable place to sit now."

Dead eyes turned his way. "The futon wasn't that bad."

Jasper rubbed his chest. This hadn't been his intention. He had wanted to fix Abel. Jasper couldn't show him weakness. He took Abel's hand. "Come here." He led Abel to the couch and sat, pulling Abel down into his lap. Abel shook in his arms. Jasper went to work, removing Abel's bowtie. After tossing the piece aside, he wrapped his arms around him and waited. Abel's muscles eventually relaxed. Jasper kissed the shell of his ear. "God. You just fucking own me." As much as Jasper hated exposing his heart, Abel needed to see it.

"I don't even know you."

That was bullshit. "Close your eyes and don't open them." As he made the command, Jasper deepened his voice the way he always had when coming to Abel as Sir. Abel closed his eyes. "I'm so proud of you." Abel took a shuttered breath at the praise. Jasper gave him more. "You could've given in to temptation when you left me, but you didn't. Instead, you looked for a healthy way to survive without me." He kissed Abel's shoulder. "You know me. I'm your biggest cheerleader. Since the first time I set eyes on you, I knew you could win." Jasper nuzzled Abel's neck. "I should punish you for running away, but I know it was my fault. You don't have to worry I'll let you down again. Do I need to worry you'll run away again?"

"No, sir."

Jasper bit back a smile. "Good. There won't be any working for you. You're mine and I've always taken care of you. Money isn't something you need to think about. I should've made sure you understood I would never let you go. To make up for that, you'll live here now. Understood?"

"Yes, sir." Abel chewed his bottom lip.

Jasper couldn't take it. "It's okay to ask questions."

Abel nodded. "Do I call you Sir or Jasper? I don't know what's real. It feels like you're two different people, but then again, it doesn't." Abel's shoulders fell. "I don't know."

"You can call me whatever you like," Jasper said while rubbing Abel's back. "This is me. Sometimes, I'm serious. Other times, I'm playful. Both times, I'm in charge. You are always my top priority. Everything I do is for you. I bought this house for you." He skimmed his lips across Abel's shoulder and spoke against his skin. "Tell me you know me."

Abel didn't hesitate. "I know you."

A ragged breath escaped Jasper. "Do you think you can open your eyes now and not be scared?"

"I don't know." The pain and honesty in Abel's voice broke Jasper's heart. He had fought so hard for Abel. Jasper needed Abel to accept all of him. Not just the mystery man who watched over him.

"Tell me what you need."

Abel's breathing turned rapid as if his nerves suddenly frayed. He sounded exactly like he walked toward the electric chair to his death and couldn't contain his fear. When he spoke, his voice shook and sounded small. "Take away my choice. Control me." His voice grew stronger. "There's something missing inside me." His eyes opened. Dark green irises focused on Jasper and didn't budge. "I need you to be that missing piece."

"Close your eyes."

Abel did as told.

The moment his eyes closed; Jasper whisked his lips across Abel's. "You don't have to worry. I'm here."

Abel swayed his way.

Jasper's heart melted at the trust Abel always silently handed him. This time, when their lips met, Abel shifted positions and straddled Jasper's lap. Kissing Abel was phenomenal. Jasper felt like he had been waiting forever to freely have this. For a moment, Jasper tolerated Abel's sweet kisses. Then he remembered Abel had begged to be controlled.

With his arms wrapped around Abel, Jasper stood. Abel wrapped his legs around Jasper like a good boy and held on as Jasper made his way down the hall.

"It's time for you to see your new bedroom."

Abel buried his face against the crook of Jasper's neck. "Thank you. I miss being held."

Jasper planned to hold Abel for the rest of his life, but first, he would get fucked. He had been pleasing Abel for too long without getting touched in return. Jasper's patience was gone. He was too controlling for most people. Being famous made things worse. He could likely fuck anyone he wanted, but he would also likely land in the news and be sued after he scared the hell out of them. Jasper didn't take risks like that. Not to mention, he had wanted no one other than Abel since the first time he saw him.

Jasper turned on the lights as he stepped into the room, and then he dimmed them. He wanted to see everything tonight. Jasper turned in a slow circle so Abel could inspect his new bedroom. Everything had been decorated with Abel in mind.

"It looks a lot like my bedroom at Silas's."

"Change isn't good for you. You need a steady life, so I tried to keep things as close as possible."

Abel met his stare. Jasper saw the realization grow in Abel's eyes. Abel saw it now. He knew Jasper hadn't lied at Assets. Jasper loved Abel. He would take care of him and keep him well. There would be no backsliding or running away. Abel would have the love and security he had been denied his entire life. He was home.

With his heart full, Jasper carried Abel to bed. After gently lowering Abel onto the bed, Jasper undressed him. Since Abel had only been wearing pants when Jasper abducted him, it wasn't hard. Once Abel was nude, Jasper stared down at him, drinking his fill. Abel still needed to gain a little more weight. He had a few bones that protruded, showing his neglect. None of that detracted from his beauty. In Jasper's eyes, he was perfect. His dark hair was a mess from running his fingers through it in his stress. Abel's dark green eyes were soft with affection as he stared at Jasper. Jasper wanted that more than he could admit to anyone.

Jasper took a step back and stripped.

Abel watched in silence. His dick hardened as if anticipating Jasper's touch.

A deep breath filled Jasper's lungs. It was the calm before the storm. He felt the darkness building inside him. There was no holding that side of him at bay. His mouth watered. He couldn't stop himself from swooping in and licking Abel's cock. Jasper loved to lick and suck. To bite. A soft moan filled the air. Jasper kissed and bit his way to Abel's mouth. He wanted to taste that sound. Their bodies molded as their tongues played. Jasper rolled his hips. A moan vibrated around his tongue. Abel's fingers dug into Jasper's back. His desire to watch overcame his need to taste.

Jasper rolled onto his back. "There's lube and condoms in the bedside table. Get them." As Abel moved to do as told, Jasper added an addendum. "I've seen your blood tests, but you haven't seen mine. You deserve to know mine are all negative, as well. I know I set no boundaries when we met, but I thought it was understood. You're not allowed to sleep with anyone else and you don't have to worry I will either. With that said, I'll leave it up to you if you want to use condoms or not. I've been sucking your dick with no barriers for months. So really, it's your decision, because I promise you, I'm the last man you'll ever sleep with."

Abel stared down at the open nightstand drawer, as if he didn't know what to do.

A thought occurred to Jasper, darkening his thoughts. "If you don't trust that you can be faithful to me then do us both a favor and use a condom."

Abel quickly grabbed only the lube.

Jasper fought an evil grin. He knew Abel. Nothing bothered Abel more than anyone seeing him as weak. He would stay faithful. Jasper motioned toward his body. "Use that lube however you need. I want to watch you sit on my cock."

The one thing Abel did with absolute confidence was take orders. When told what to do, Abel set to work without hesitation. He popped open the lube and oiled Jasper's cock. As Abel straddled Jasper's hips, Jasper fought the urge to haul him upward and suck his dick instead. Abel was delicious. He was such an addiction for Jasper. Jasper forced himself to stay still. His reward was the sensation of Abel swiping Jasper's crown across his asshole, prepping Abel. Then Abel pushed himself down on Jasper's dick. Jasper's stomach caved and his spine curved. Abel moved slowly, no doubt taking things easy since it had been a long time. Jasper hauled Abel down and claimed his mouth. He held Abel's jaw in a tight grip and sucked his tongue. Abel panted. Jasper pushed him away, setting Abel free to use Jasper in any way he needed. Abel lifted slightly and sat. Jasper's spine bowed. He couldn't help it. His mind knew it was Abel on his cock. The tight heat was killing him. Then Abel found his pace and Jasper couldn't look away. He touched Abel every place he could reach while Abel rode him. Jasper tugged Abel's dick, needing Abel to feel good.

Abel moaned and gasped as he used Jasper's body. When Abel blew, Jasper lost his ability to stay passive. He rolled, pinning Abel beneath him. He pumped and thrust, using Abel's asshole the way he liked. Abel clawed at Jasper's skin and cried Jasper's name. Something about hearing his real name tearing from Abel's throat shook him. His crazed motions slowed. He held Abel's jaw, forcing Abel to hold his stare while Jasper made love to him.

As Jasper's balls drew up tight and the pressure beat at his crown, Jasper's connection with Abel deepened. "I love you." The confession tore from him on a gasp as he pumped Abel's ass full of cum. His body shook and his heart raced, but Jasper felt calmer than he had in ages. This was right. Jasper was where he belonged.

·♥·♥·♥·♥·♥·

There was a stillness about the air that Abel hadn't felt in a long time. He felt human. Normal. Happy. That was all due to Jasper. Jasper held him. He petted Abel and played footsie with him beneath the covers. Their fingers toyed with each other. Abel felt free.

"I have questions."

Jasper's gaze locked on to Abel, as if there was nothing he wasn't willing to talk about. "Okay."

"Why wasn't I allowed to touch you?"

A sweet smile touched Jasper's lips. Every second that ticked by Abel realized a little more how real Jasper was. This was Sir. This was the man he had wanted to have just like this, but he had been too scared to admit it, even to himself.

"The simple answer is I didn't want you to know anything identifying about me."

"What's the complicated answer?"

Jasper traced the line of Abel's jaw with his fingertip. "I was scared I would fail you, but I'd still end up wanting you just like this, and then I'd fail me too."

That was fair. Abel was scared as hell every day that he would slip and go back to being a junkie. Now he had to fear taking Jasper down with him too. It was a huge responsibility. "You shouldn't have risked your sobriety on me. I'm not worth it."

Jasper's expression hardened. "Don't say that again." When Abel didn't respond, Jasper swatted his ass. "I didn't hear your agreement."

"Yes, sir."

He felt Jasper relax. "That's better."

Abel couldn't take it. "Why did you, though? I mean, what made you take a chance on me?" There was nothing special about Abel, but he didn't add that part.

For a moment, Jasper stared at nothing, as if thinking of the past or deeply considering Abel's question. "I didn't intend to," he said after a moment, surprising Abel. Luckily, he didn't leave it at that. "When Silas called and asked me to come take a look at one of his pets, I was annoyed as hell. He knows how I feel about going to parties like his where the alcohol is flowing, but I owed him. I planned to show up, take a cursory glance, and leave." Jasper smiled. "Then I saw you."

Abel snorted. "I was so gone. I don't remember a single thing about that night."

Jasper nodded. "I'm not surprised. You struck me, though. Despite being out of your head, you had a rage about you—like you wanted to live but didn't know how. I couldn't leave you like that. Still, I planned to send you to rehab and not look back. But I did. That first time I visited you after you got out of rehab, I should've known it was over for me." Jasper took an audible breath. It was ragged and sexy. "You were so submissive and perfect. You questioned nothing I did or asked of you. Being with you is freeing as hell. For me, staying sober means never relinquishing control. Not many people would let me have what you do."

For the first time in Abel's life, purpose filled his chest. He had never felt important or like he fit anywhere. His place was with Jasper. The world had never made more sense than it did in that moment. Heat unexpectedly filled Abel's cheeks as another question ate at his brain. He had to know, though. "I always wondered, why the blow jobs with no type of reciprocation? You got nothing from your visits with me."

A sexy laugh rumbled from Jasper, making the muscles tighten in Abel's stomach. "That's not true at all. If you haven't noticed, I have a huge oral fixation." Jasper swept a heated gaze down Abel's body. "That's why I required you to send me the results from all your STD tests. Sucking dick and drinking cum is an absolute must for me."

Abel fought the urge to cover his face. He knew it had to be red. "Then I guess it's a good thing I was always more worried about getting high than getting laid."

"Mhmm," Jasper said, sounding noncommittal. "I think you should kiss me so I can get back to using my tongue."

While fighting a smile, Abel scrambled to do as told. He still couldn't believe this was real, but—as their tongues met—Abel knew he would accept everything Jasper offered nonetheless, because Jasper was right. Abel knew him. With his eyes closed and Jasper's hands on his body, Abel recognized Sir and all the fantasies he had given Abel. Abel recalled every time he wished for more and realized now he would have it. He wouldn't back down or run from this. Not that Jasper would let him anyhow. It was funny how that knowledge made him smile. Maybe he was a bit fucked.

Chapter Eight

♥

ABEL FOLDED HIS CLOTHES and packed his bags. He moved from the bathroom to the bedroom, grabbing toiletries and dumping those in his bag too. Abel didn't have a lot at Silas's place, but he had more than he realized. Thankfully, Jasper had brought a few suitcases for Abel to fill while he settled things with Silas. Abel was more than a little nervous about that. He chewed his bottom lip while he packed. No doubt Silas was a bit angry over the way things had shaken out. He couldn't picture Jasper apologizing to anyone either. It was possible he might not be welcomed back. That was depressing since Abel's brother lived here.

"So, you're really taking him back."

Abel jumped at Kage's sudden appearance in the open doorway. His nerves were more frayed than he realized. "Dang. You startled me." Abel patted his chest, trying to slow his heart. Since Kage had rescued him, Abel felt he deserved an explanation. "Yeah. I think I have to. Jasper pulled me from the edge of death and brought me back to life. I suppose that sounds dramatic, but it's true. He deserves a second chance."

Kage nodded. He didn't look convinced, but he also didn't argue. Kage didn't move deeper into the room. Abel hated Kage was obviously upset with him. He fought a sigh. Most people wouldn't understand. Abel needed what only Jasper could give him. He chose to change the subject.

"What has you here today?"

Kage's shoulders relaxed a hair. "Silas has some workers coming in to do a bit of remodeling. He asked me to guard Benji's door while they're here."

"What's up with that?"

At Abel's question, Kage shrugged and shuffled into the room. "I don't know. Silas pays me and I don't ask questions."

Abel nodded. He supposed it wasn't his business anyhow.

Kage moved to the chair and sat.

Abel fought a smile. He knew Kage wouldn't touch that chair if he knew anything about it.

Thankfully, Kage spoke and saved Abel from telling on himself. "A lot of things in this house aren't my business, but I hope you know I'll be around if you need me."

Abel stopped packing and focused on Kage. "Thank you. I hope you know I appreciate everything you've done for me. Not many people have come to my rescue over the years. I won't forget that."

Kage nodded and looked around. He rubbed the back of his neck. "So you're moving on. Where are you headed? Doesn't Jasper live in Vegas?"

"He bought a house down the street so life could be as steady as possible for me."

A hint of a smile touched Kage's lips. Abel imagined it could mean anything. "That's good. Can I help with anything?"

"He's good, but thank you," Jasper said, strolling into the room as if he owned the place—like he did everywhere he went.

Kage rolled his eyes and stood. He headed for the door.

Jasper called out, stopping him. "By the way, Kage. I appreciate you taking Abel home with you the other night. Without your help, he might've end up doing anything. So, thank you."

With a dip of his chin, Kage walked away, leaving them alone. Abel fought a smile. He doubted Jasper thanked people often. Once they were alone, Jasper turned Abel's way. A slow and wicked-looking smile stretched his lips.

"He sat in that chair."

Abel covered his mouth and snorted.

Jasper's eyes danced with laughter. Then, unexpectedly, he sprang. Jasper took Abel down on the bed and kissed every place he could reach while Abel squealed with laughter. His stomach hurt. Abel never laughed anymore. He was out of practice. With a loud sigh, Jasper pushed Abel's suitcase out of the way and rolled to the side. He tossed one leg over Abel, keeping him pinned to the bed.

"Are you sad to be leaving?"

Abel thought it over. "No. Not really. This has never felt like home. Obviously, I like seeing my brother all the time. It's given us a chance to grow closer, but I've always known I was only a guest here." He turned his head and met Jasper's stare. "Plus, you're not here. I want to be with you."

Jasper leaned in and kissed Abel. Their lips clung as they shared each other's air. "I love you," Jasper whispered against his lips.

Abel's heart melted every time Jasper said those words. His chest warmed. Abel wanted to say them back, but he was scared he didn't mean them. No one had taught him how to love. Abel had been born into rage and pain. He didn't understand healthy love. It made him sad not to give Jasper the words he deserved. Abel just wanted to know he meant them.

As always, he swore Jasper read his mind. He stroked Abel's cheek. "Don't worry. I don't expect you to return my words. I just need you to know you're loved."

Abel bumped noses with him. Jasper pressed his forehead against Abel's.

Abel's throat swelled. He had never felt this way before. There was this constant fear sitting on his chest. He didn't want to lose this man who had saved him when everyone else had turned their backs.

A light knock landed on the open door. Abel turned his head and spotted his brother in the doorway. Jasper helped him sit up and Abel pasted on a smile. He would do whatever it took to keep Jasper. Someday soon, he would deserve the man who had risked everything on him.

·♥·♥·♥·♥·♥·

Jasper stayed out of the way and smiled a lot while Abel visited with his brother. It had been a strange day.

Jasper wasn't used to humbling himself. First, he had been forced to apologize to Silas, since Silas had been beyond enraged over Jasper tricking Abel. He had chosen to forgive Jasper for Abel's sake. Then Jasper had decided to thank Kage, even though it grated. He recognized Kage had kept Abel clean in a moment he was at his weakest. Jasper hoped not to have another morning like this one. He wasn't good at playing nice with others.

Soon, this place would be behind him, as he thought it had been years ago. He couldn't forget Abel's brother still lived here. Jasper wanted Abel to have a relationship with Griffin. Every tie Abel had would make him stronger. Griffin helped them carry bags and luggage down the street, moving Abel's things in one trip.

Jasper left Abel alone to give Griffin the tour. He didn't want Abel to feel strange about making the place his own. Jasper had no clue how long Griffin stayed. He changed into his gym shorts, wrapped his knuckles, and disappeared inside his home gym. He bounced in place and beat his speed bag before moving on to his heavy bag. Time passed while his mind blanked. Jasper needed these decompressing moments.

Jasper's mom had passed when Jasper was three. His dad had been a trainer for a local gym. While he hadn't trained any US champions, he had still churned out some decent boxers. His dad hadn't known how to be soft and so Jasper hadn't learned either. All Jasper had ever known was strict discipline. His father had died of a heart attack alone in his gym. He hadn't lived to see Jasper become anything more than an alcoholic. That was when Jasper decided to turn his life around. He had been determined to reach the highest level possible. Jasper thought he would feel complete when he won his title. He hadn't known real peace until he met Abel.

Jasper's muscles burned. Sweat rolled down his back. He took a break to grab some water. When he turned, he found Abel asleep on the mat feet away. A smile exploded across Jasper's face. Abel was so quietly needy. It was adorable. Jasper never got enough. After grabbing a towel, Jasper wiped away as much sweat as he could. Then he bent and lifted Abel from the floor. Abel woke up long enough to settle into Jasper's arms and then he was out again. It took longer than people realized to recover from years of killing a body. In some ways, Abel was still healing. He needed sleep, food, water, and love. Jasper had everything Abel would ever want.

He tucked Abel into bed and hurried through a shower. When he returned to the bedroom, Abel was still asleep. Jasper eased into bed next to Abel. Abel rolled into his arms. Even though Jasper wasn't the least bit tired, he snuggled close and closed his eyes. This was the life Jasper had always wanted. He planned to enjoy it.

Chapter Nine

♥

JASPER: *There's no charge on the card for lunch.*

Abel: *I stayed home and made a salad. I don't feel good today.*

Jasper: *Give me ten minutes. I'll cut training short and come cuddle you.*

Abel: *You don't have to do that.*

Jasper: *Yes. I do.*

·♥·♥·♥·♥·♥·

Abel: *Andrew's art studio opens tonight and they're having a grand opening thing. I'd like to go.*

Jasper: *That's fine. I'll be home soon. We can head out then.*

Abel: *Yay. See you soon.*

· ♥ · ♥ · ♥ · ♥ · ♥ ·

Jasper: *I have to go to Vegas. You should start packing.*

Abel: *Okay.*

Jasper: *Good boy.*

·♥·♥·♥·♥·♥·

Living in Vegas had been a lot more convenient than New Orleans, but Jasper still believed the move was worthwhile. That didn't mean he didn't have to make the trip to do various things occasionally. He wouldn't be going without Abel any longer. The penthouse they were staying in had an amazing view of the skyline at night. Abel hadn't left the balcony since the sun had set. Jasper couldn't take his eyes off him.

Abel glanced over and caught Jasper staring. He smiled. "It's beautiful here. I've never been to Vegas before."

"You're beautiful."

Abel smiled, curled his nose, and looked away. Even though Abel never argued with him, he always looked disbelieving when Jasper complimented him. Jasper hated that.

He couldn't take it. "You genuinely don't think you're hot, do you?"

Abel shrugged at the question. "I didn't really get the looks in the family. Those went to my little brother."

Jasper didn't believe that, but he saw Abel did. He understood, though. That was the thing about constant abuse. Eventually, nothing looked beautiful any longer, especially yourself. "I wish you could see what I do when I look at you. You take my breath."

A small smile touched Abel's lips, but he said nothing.

"You should marry me."

That got Abel's attention. His gaze snapped to Jasper's. For a moment, he eyed Jasper, as if assessing his seriousness. "Is that what you want?"

Jasper didn't miss a beat. "It is, but this one time, I won't demand it of you. I'm asking. There's a lot I'll force to have my way, but I don't want to marry someone who doesn't want to marry me."

Abel looked away. He stared at the skyline, looking lost in thought. His silence was killing Jasper. In the three months Abel had been living with Jasper, Abel had grown by leaps and bounds under Jasper's care. This one time, much like not commanding Abel to say he loved him, he wouldn't force

Abel to marry him. Some things he needed Abel to do for himself, so Jasper knew it was real. The longer the quiet went on between them, the more Jasper lost hope. Abel still hadn't confessed any feelings of love. Likely Jasper shouldn't have asked for more without those words. He never expected to feel insecure in their relationship. Jasper was getting there now as the silence grew.

"Am I stealing you away from this place?"

Jasper wasn't expecting Abel to counter his question with a question. "No. We're sitting here right now."

Abel didn't laugh or look his way. "Sometimes, I think about telling you how much I love you, then I remember who you are and who I am. It seems wrong for me to steal you from the amazing life you could have without me."

Jasper wanted to be enraged, but he had said he would let Abel choose. Also, Abel had admitted to loving him and Jasper needed that. But Abel's confession made him realize he might be failing Abel in some ways. "I had this before I met you. It didn't make me happy. This place is just a town. My title is just a title. Everything about my life felt cold, and I knew something was missing. Then I met you and—for the first time—I've found something I can't live without. You're right. You are too good for me, but I'm still hoping you'll stay in the gutter with me and marry me anyhow."

Abel finally looked his way. "That's not what I meant, and you know it, but I won't argue."

"Good," Jasper growled, letting Abel know he skated a thin line.

Abel smiled. It was sweet and had Jasper hungry to taste him. "I love you."

Jasper drew a steadying breath. A small part of him had thought he wouldn't hear those words from Abel. "I love you too."

"I'd be honored to marry you." Abel made the claim so calm and sure that it caught Jasper off guard for a second. He didn't react right away.

When Abel's words sank in, Jasper shot to his feet. He couldn't believe Abel had agreed, but there would be no going back. Abel smiled up at him as Jasper came to stand over him. Before even Jasper knew what he would do, Jasper snatched Abel from his chair and tossed him over his shoulder. Abel laughed as Jasper headed for the elevator. It wasn't until the door opened and Jasper stepped inside that Abel questioned him.

"Wait. Where are we going? I thought you were taking me to bed."

Jasper caressed Abel's ass because he could. "Not yet, baby. I know you. You're a runner. I'm not taking any chances."

"What?" Abel sounded confused as hell. Jasper didn't enlighten him.

When the elevator opened on the first floor, he strolled out through the crowd with Abel over his shoulder and zero fucks. People knew his face here. Phones appeared in people's hands as they openly took pictures and video of Jasper carrying Abel through the hotel. A smile that felt evil even to him stretched his lips. This would be all over the internet in no time. Let them talk. He wanted everyone to know he belonged to Abel and Abel belonged to him. He carried Abel straight into the wedding chapel attached to the hotel. Jasper didn't set Abel on his feet until he had finished arranging everything. Despite looking like he might faint, Abel signed everything set in front of him, repeated his vows, and kissed Jasper when they were pronounced husbands for life. For a man who had achieved some of the biggest dreams known to man, it was the greatest moment of Jasper's life.

·♥·♥·♥·♥·♥·

To say Abel was shell-shocked would be the understatement of a lifetime. In the back of his mind, beneath the shock, Abel recognized Jasper was right to marry Abel the minute he agreed. When it came to marriage, Abel was a runner. It terrified him to think of anyone tied to his poison for life. Jasper had taken away that time to overthink.

Still, Abel rode the elevator back to their room looking down at his hand at a ring that had magically appeared from Jasper's pocket—like he had planned this all along. Abel didn't know whether he should hyperventilate or climb Jasper like a tree. So many holy shits kept hitting him. He was married. Abel had married Sir. He had fucking married the goddamn US middleweight boxing champion. What the fuck had happened to his life? The elevator door opened, and Jasper had to lead him out. Abel's legs still didn't want to work.

"Are you okay? You don't look happy."

Abel's gaze jumped to Jasper's face at Jasper's claim. He had married this really amazing person. A smile spread across his lips. It was out of his control. "We're married."

Jasper nodded. "We really are."

A laugh escaped Abel, forcing him to cover his mouth. For a moment, he stared at Jasper, awed. Jasper was completely nuts for marrying him. Abel wouldn't point it out, though.

Jasper looked a bit unsure of himself. "Say something."

Abel dropped his hand and made a helpless motion. "I'm so happy, I don't know where to start."

"You should start by kissing me."

Abel didn't hesitate walking into Jasper's arms. When their lips met, the truth slammed into Abel. He would never again be who he was before

Jasper came into his life. This was forever. Jasper would never let him go backward. His throat swelled. He had crossed a line into a new and healthy territory. It was all due to Jasper.

"Take off your pants."

A laugh burst from Abel at the abruptness of Jasper's demand, but he didn't hesitate to do as told. Even when he stood completely nude in front of a still fully dressed Jasper, Abel didn't feel weak. A sudden realization overcame Abel as Jasper dropped to his knees. Since the first time Jasper had touched him like this, Jasper had been showing Abel something Abel refused to see. Even though Jasper was the one in control, Abel owned him. Jasper belonged to Abel through and through.

Abel ran his fingers through Jasper's hair while Jasper kissed his stomach. His eyes burned as he was overcome by how powerful their relationship truly was. They were equal in a way he hadn't recognized. They completed each other. Their cracks fit together, making one perfect soul. This was meant to be.

Jasper's gaze met Abel's as he swallowed Abel's cock. Abel's knees weakened from more than just the pleasure. Love washed over him along with the knowledge he would never be alone again. Jasper was his family. They were perfect.

Chapter Ten

♥

ONE OF SILAS' CRAZY parties raged a floor beneath Kage. He was bored off his ass. Guarding Benji's door was easy money. Silas paid him a lot to do nothing all night. Still, sometimes he missed having a life. The feeling lasted less than fifteen seconds. That was how long it took him to remember that all men were liars and cheats. Working security for Assets got him all the free ass a guy could want. He didn't need anything more permanent. Money brought way more happiness.

The door opened behind him, hitting Kage in the back and pulling him from his thoughts. He hastened to check behind the door. Benji was on his knees with toilet paper held to his nose. It was obvious he was bleeding profusely.

Kage dropped to his haunches. "Are you okay?"

Benji stared at him with pain and tears in his eyes. "Could you get my daddy, please?"

"Of course." Kage shot to his feet and pulled out his phone. He shot a quick 911 text to Silas.

Silas was at the top of the stairs before Kage put his phone away.

"What's wrong?" Silas asked, bypassing Kage and going straight for where

Benji sat on his knees.

Through the door, Kage heard Benji's muffled response. "I woke up and couldn't remember where I was, and I fell."

Kage's heart squeezed in his chest.

Silas made a soothing sound. "It's okay, sweet angel. I've got you." Silas peeked around the door. "I'll stay with him. If you're willing, I'll pay you double for tonight to keep an eye on things downstairs. I have security, of course, but you're who I trust to take my place."

Kage couldn't pretend he wasn't moved by Silas' words. "No problem. Just take care of Benji. I've got things covered."

Kage saw the mixture of relief and concern in Silas's eyes. He needed help tonight. Kage had his back. It took every ounce of his willpower to turn away from the image of Silas caring for Benji. There was so much love between them. They needed him downstairs. That knowledge had Kage jogging down the steps.

Honestly, he had no idea what Silas needed him to do. Kage decided to pretend he was on bouncer duty at Assets. He kept an eye on the guys in costume and in cages, ensuring they were safe. Everyone seemed fine. He had learned not to judge years ago. Every single person on the planet was just trying to survive life. Sometimes, that meant stepping into roles other people didn't understand. All the people here would likely go to a regular job on Monday with no one the wiser to their lifestyle. Meanwhile, they had survived a little longer. That was all that mattered.

As Kage weaved through the crowd, someone stepped into his path. It was a tiny blond beauty in a cat costume. His baby blue eyes flashed with mischief as he handed Kage a rose. When Kage automatically accepted, a blush made the cat's eyes stand out even more. He turned away and slipped into the crowd before Kage could react. Too late, he realized he was smiling as he brought the rose to his nose. It had been a strange night.

·♥·♥·♥·♥·♥·

Hand in hand, Jasper and Abel walked down the sidewalk. Jasper saw Andrew and Griffin waiting for them up ahead. Behind them, security worked the gate. Jasper shook his head. It seemed like Silas's parties were getting closer together all the time.

Abel skipped ahead, dragging Jasper along in his wake as he raced to get to Griffin. The brothers embraced while Jasper and Andrew nodded at each other.

Abel pulled away and motioned toward the house. "I see Silas is having a party. Why aren't you working?"

Griffin shrugged. "My brother got married. We have to go celebrate."

Jasper smiled as he watched the pair chatting and Abel showing off his wedding band. He wanted the brothers to have a good relationship.

Andrew steered the group away from the house, heading toward the river. "How was Vegas, besides the obvious?"

Jasper shrugged. "Not bad. I had some contract shit to clear up. How's the new studio coming along?"

"Better than expected." As a group, they headed toward a nearby restaurant while chatting about nothing of real importance. It struck Jasper. They were family now. A weird warmth spread through his chest as they commandeered an outdoor table. He had been alone in the world for so long, he hadn't thought much about how it would feel to have an extended family again. It was nice. His gaze moved Abel's way as he invaded Abel's space, leaving him barely any room to breathe. Abel's eyes danced with laughter as he let Jasper be as obnoxious as possible. It was such a small gesture that mattered not at all to anyone other than Jasper. To Jasper, getting to be whatever version of himself that woke up that day meant everything.

"Awwww." At Griffin's long, drawn-out cooing, Jasper tore his gaze away from Abel to focus on Griffin. Griffin smiled unrepentantly. "You two look so in love. It makes me smile."

Jasper's gaze slid back toward his smiling husband. "We are in love."

Abel's smile grew even brighter at Jasper's proclamation. Jasper's hand moved to Abel's thigh and slid upward. Abel visibly fought not to look his way. An evil chuckle rose in Jasper's throat. Happiness had him feeling too much, and he planned to make it Abel's problem. He sipped his drink to hide a laugh as he slid his hand even higher. They should get together with family more often. Jasper could definitely picture spending the rest of his life just like this.

Keep an eye out for the next book in the 'D' series, *Guardian*.

Please consider leaving a review at the retailer where you purchased this book. Reviews really help with a book's visibility, which allows me to continue writing more stories. Thank you, Charity.

About the Author

♥

CHARITY PARKERSON IS AN award-winning and multi-published author with several companies. Born with no filter from her brain to her mouth, she decided to take this odd quirk and insert it in her characters.

*Eight-time Readers' Favorite Award Winner

*2015 Passionate Plume Award Finalist

*2013 Reviewers' Choice Award Winner

*2012 ARRA Finalist for Favorite Paranormal Romance

*Five-time winner of The Mistress of the Darkpath

Connect with her online:

—Sign up for my newsletter: https://sendfox.com/charityparkerson

—Join my readers' group on Facebook: http://bit.ly/CharitysTribe

—Website: charityparkerson.com

—Facebook:
facebook.com/authorCharityParkerson
facebook.com/TheMenofSin—Twitter:
twitter.com/CharityParkerso

—Instagram:
Instagram.com/sinnerauthor

—Bookbub:
https://www.bookbub.com/authors/charity-parkerson

—Amazon page: author.to/

—TikTok:
http://www.tiktok.com/@charityparkerson